Evasive Maneuvers

Will they find the love behind the lies?

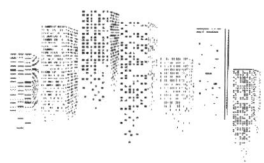

LYNN MICHAELS

Copyright © 2016 Lynn Michaels & Rubicon Fiction
Blue Eyed Dreams, LLC
All rights reserved.
ISBN: 1532907931
ISBN-13: 978-1532907937

DEDICATION

To Amy - thanks for pushing me to make my stories better.
To Maggie - thanks for making me laugh at myself.
To Melissa - welcome to the team.

Contents

1 Campbell	1
2 Stone	13
3 Campbell	20
4 Stone	37
5 Campbell	41
6 Stone	46
7 Campbell	53
8 Stone	60
9 Campbell	67
10 Stone	69
11 Campbell	73
12 Stone	77
13 Campbell	84
14 Stone	90
15 Campbell	95
16 Stone	104
17 Campbell	111
18 Stone	119
19 Campbell	122
20 Stone	126
21 Campbell	131
22 Stone	136
23 Campbell	144
24 Stone	153
25 Campbell	160
26 Stone	169
27 Campbell	173
28 Stone	178
Bonus Scene...	184
Evasive Maneuvers Playlist	190

ACKNOWLEDGMENTS

Devil In the Details Editing
Simply Defined Art

1 Campbell

I walked into the club with my serious *I'm hot shit* attitude, strutting my stuff. Club Dragon resided in the middle of Ybor City where it waited for Saturday night and all the regulars to come and hang out. Though it should seem like the same old same old, I had a good vibe going on, invigorating me and making everything new. Like any other Saturday night out, my skinny-jeans—practically painted on—and my tight t-shirt—torn in all the right places—showed off my best assets. As soon as I stepped inside, the music pounded through my body, reverberating in my chest and pulsing right down through my balls, feeling like an anthem and begging me to dance.

My friend Julien headed to the bar with a wave, knowing I had to sweat it out on the dance floor before I even started drinking. "Later, Camp!" he called as we parted, walking through our roles like a play we'd put on a million times before, completely comfortable with our lines and hitting our marks.

The strobe lights flashed and pulsed with the music as I stepped out into the throng of hot bodies jumping and grinding with the beat. The whole floor moved like one massive monster, gyrating and turning to the tune, like rats following the piper to their doom. I joined them anyway, my body moving of its own accord, and glanced over the others on the floor. That's when I saw him across the room.

He swayed a little out of tune with the music as if he

heard some different, dissonant beat in his head. I'd never seen anything like him. He had a tough attitude, uncaring and so far from the self-absorbed club rats I normally ended up with, and so unlike me. He wore his dark hair cut short around the sides with tight curls across the top—not even highlighted, but left a natural oaky brown. His eyes pierced me from across the dance floor, though I couldn't tell the color from this distance and the house lights that played across him. He wore tight jeans and an unzipped hoodie that exposed his bare chest. Just a smattering of dark hair spilled across his pecks and a small line flowed down his ripped abdomen in a treasure trail that disappeared into the waistband of his jeans. My ass clenched tight, imagining him inside me, thrusting his hard cock, slowly in and out.

    I had to get him to notice me, to take me seriously, to think I'm different from all those other guys who were dancing up on him, hitting on him, grabbing his ass and flicking their greedy fingers across that god-like chest. He'd grabbed my attention like no other, leaving me desperate to prove myself, but I had a hard time coming up with one thing about me that he'd find interesting or different. What did I have to offer this guy? He so obviously didn't fit in this club, though he hardly knew it. More than likely, I'd drag him down, if I even had a shot at him.

    I made my way across the floor, frantically grasping for something I could say. I had an abundance of attitude and could be a barrel of fun, but neither of those things were going to impress this guy. He seemed self-assured, willing and able to tell anyone who didn't agree to fuck off. The way he moved, the way he looked around, taking in the scene, all screamed that he was made of something more than the rest of us and certainly more than me.

    I graduated from community college with an Associate degree and had a halfway decent job in the file room of a big corporation. My dad had given me a nice car when I graduated, but I didn't have it in me to go back to school and truly earn the damn thing. I could never be a lawyer like my old man. I was too alternative with my tattoos and piercings, the gauge in my left ear and my in-your-face gayness, but the hottie in the hoodie didn't know any of that.

When I stood in front of him—all in his space—refusing to move, he looked at me. A kaleidoscope of color swirled through his eyes and his full lips trembled, begging me to kiss him, but I didn't. I just shifted my hips, daring him to dance with me. His shoulders were broader than mine and he was just a tiny bit taller than me. I had a long lean torso, while his was stocky and well-muscled, but not bulky like a gym bunny either. He obviously lifted, but didn't overdo it and probably got just as much cardio in, though his thighs were thick with his jeans stretched tightly over them.

He found my rhythm and matched it, putting his hands on my hips and smirking at me, taking my challenge. I smiled knowingly, but I wore a mask, part of the attitude.

We danced as the music rolled into a different melody; he pulled me closer. Want curled in my belly and sweat trickled down my back as our bodies pressed together. He rocked his hips into me, grinding against my crotch, and I couldn't help but press back. I leaned in and whispered loudly in his ear, "Wanna get outta here?"

I pulled away and looked into his eyes, his face showed hesitation.

I bit at the inside of my mouth, hoping I hadn't moved too fast. "To talk?" I asked, clarifying. Even though I really wanted him in my bed, I also wanted more than a one-night trick. Even a dumbass like me could tell this guy was something special. I could feel it thrumming through my body from my curling toes to my wanton cock to my burning ears and I hadn't even had the first drink.

"Coffee?" he mouthed. I nodded with a cocky grin. He entwined his fingers with mine and let a smile unfurl across his sweet face.

Outside, the humid night threatened to burst out into a rain storm. We walked quickly toward the corner road. "There's a great 24-hour place just a few blocks south. Coffee

Kraze. Have you heard of it?"

He nodded. "Uh-huh. I'm from around here. You?"

I gave him my most seductive smile. "Yes. I'm Campbell Fain."

"I'm Stone Medlock."

"Stone?" It sounded like a porn name, but I sure as hell wasn't going to tell him that. I simply lifted my right eyebrow in question—a trick I learned back in high school, thanks to my buddy Julien. We'd decided to learn how to do it after being enthralled by the Rock; we stayed up all night practicing. Julien never mastered the one eye-brow like I had, but he'd mastered other things I'd never do, like having a respectable job and a parent who was actually proud of him.

"Yep. That's me," he said, blushing. *OhmyGod so sweet*. My stomach flipped over at how adorable that blush looked on his sexy face. "My mom. She had a thing for those cheesy daytime soaps. She named me after one of her favorite characters. You have no idea how hard it's been growing up. Kids are fucking mean. But damn, I think my brothers had it worse. She named them Blaze and Harley."

"*OhmyGod* that's worse. Poor guys. I can just imagine the teasing. So, couldn't you go by your middle name or something?"

"Ha! No middle name. Just Stone."

"Okay, Stone. I kinda like it." That was true, I thought he looked like a Stone with his chiseled jaw, sharp cheekbones, and those hard eyes. "I think it's fitting."

He snorted. "Guess maybe I grew into it."

Oh, yes he had! I could imagine elementary school must have been tough for him. Even in high school he'd be ridiculed, but he seemed so confident now, as if any ribbing he'd gotten had rolled right off him.

"Well, Stone. What do you do?"

"Ha!" he scoffed.

Before he could really answer the question, we'd arrived at the coffee shop with the big blue and brown neon CK sign. I held the glass door open for him and followed him to the counter. He ordered a plain coffee and so did I, pleased that he didn't order one of the frou-frou drinks they offered. I paid for the coffee and we took our paper cups to the condiment counter and doctored them up. I added just a little sugar, but Stone added cinnamon and milk along with his sugar. He caught me watching him and smirked. I had to chuckle, he was so damn cute with his smug grin.

We picked a booth in the back of the restaurant, but the whole place was quiet since it was so late. "So?" I asked, hoping to get him to talk about himself some more.

He sipped his coffee a minute and then looked up at me. Under the fluorescent lights of the coffee shop his eyes twinkled a hazel brown with golden flecks that totally mesmerized me. His little pink tongue peeked out, licking his bottom lip, before he answered. "Mostly, I'm a PA for this executive guy downtown, but uh, I've done some modeling."

His confession made me choke on my coffee, especially after my porn name thoughts from earlier. "What?"

"Right, huh. I was in an Old Navy commercial. Wearing those stupid short-shorts. I kind of hated it though."

"Shorts? Short-shorts? You mean Chubbies?" That eyebrow of mine notched itself up again.

Stone laughed. "Yeah. Those."

I shook my head. "You must have great legs."

Stone shrugged. "It paid well, but it wasn't my thing."

"Oh. What is your thing? What do you do as a PA?"

After a long slow sip of coffee, he moaned a little, making my already half-hard cock grow even more and press painfully against my jeans.

He eyed me as if he knew what was going on in my pants. "This and that. Whatever he needs done. Running errands. Data entry. Keeping his schedule."

"Sounds boring."

"I don't know. It's okay. What do you do?"

"I'm a law student. Working as an intern in my dad's firm, Fain, Montgomery, Forsyth. I'm sure you've heard of it." The lie spilled out of my mouth like water over rocks in a stream.

Stone seemed so down to earth, so real, making me need to impress him even more. If I could be somebody special, he'd want my number, maybe something more than just a hot fuck. He'd want more than a file clerk, club rat, fucking disappointment to my semi-famous father and the rest of the world. The lie was only a half-truth. My dad really was *that* Fain and I could be going to law school, if I wanted.

"Oh, that Fain? Really? Yeah, I've heard of it. Mr. St. James uses your firm."

"St. James?"

"That's who I work for." He took another long sip of his coffee. I'd hardly touched mine. The bitter coffee didn't taste quite so good with the lie still fresh on my tongue.

"Oh. Well, it's a pretty big firm." I suddenly wondered if my dad would really give me a job if I enrolled in school. But I didn't want to be a lawyer, I just wanted to impress Stone.

Stone glanced at my coffee. He probably wondered why I wasn't drinking it. That prompted a few good sips from me. Silence sat between us, but not uncomfortably. Stone broke the quiet with a brave face. "So, do you have to take all that out when you work?"

"What?"

Stone grabbed at his ears, nodding toward me.

"Oh, the gauge and the piercings? Well, no, but I don't meet with clients or anything. I'm behind the scenes. Really low level." Right, I worked the file room, just at another company, but I couldn't say that. I needed to play it down, didn't want to get carried away. "Good coffee, huh?" I held my half empty cup up in a gesture that I hoped would change the subject without being too obvious.

"Sure, I like it. I come here a good deal." He took another sip, then his dark brows pushed together above his nose, wrinkling up in thought and making me want to kiss the creases away until he relaxed again. "That's pretty cool, following in your dad's footsteps and all. I bet you'll be an awesome lawyer some day."

I had nothing to say to that. I knew it would never

happen. I almost laughed thinking that I would actually be a lawyer. Instead, I sipped my coffee, hoping for a subject change.

Stone finally broke the moment of awkward silence. "So, why haven't I seen you around? Where did you go to school?"

As locals, we should have swam in some similar circles, but Julien and I weren't like regular kids. That part of my history was true. "I went to private schools. Me and Julien. Oh, fuck!"

"What?"

"I ditched my friend at the club. Hang on and let me text him." I whipped out my phone and tapped the screen, popping off a quick text. It didn't take long for an affirmative response in the form of a thumbs up emoticon. "Cool."

"Everything's okay?"

I smiled. Julien had probably found his own hook up. "Yeah. Jay-Jay and I went to school together. A couple of trust fund brats." Again, another partial lie fell from my mouth. Julien had a trust fund, but I sure didn't. My dad wanted me to earn my way like he did and my mom spent his money faster than he could god-damned earn it anyway. I shrugged it off.

Stone looked down at his coffee as if debating whether he would drink more, those lines in the center of his brow deepening. I wanted them gone. "Hey," I said, getting his attention.

"What?" He looked up at me with those demanding hazel eyes.

"He's like my brother. We always stick together. Prep school kids are just as fucking mean as any other. Hell, I grew up looking like a fag and Jay-Jay always had my back. There has never been anything other than deep friendship between us."

"Okay." That sexy little smirk flicked across his lips and I breathed easier as his brow smoothed out. I liked his face so much better that way.

I smiled back at him. "So? What now?"

Stone leaned forward and stared at me intently, as if

studying every feature of my face in an almost challenging way. Reflexively, I leaned back, looking up at him through my bleached-blond bangs. Stone tentatively lifted his finger toward my face and I closed my eyes as he pushed my hair back. He breathed out harshly and said, "Your eyes are spectacular."

Something strange tumbled around in my stomach with his words. I didn't think I'd ever had comments on my eyes; they were ordinary. I wanted those fake colored contacts my senior year, but Julien had talked me out of them. My eyes were just a regular flat brown—ordinary.

Before I could comment, Stone smiled in a mischievous kind of way and added, "You really are exquisite."

I bit my bottom lip. This close to Stone, and his sultry compliments, made me too nervous and off my game. I didn't know how to answer him, especially since I thought he was so much better looking than me. Just one more thing to worry about and fake my way through.

"I like you, Campbell," he said flatly.

"Camp. Really, my friends just call me Camp."

"Oh. I like Campbell better."

I didn't think it mattered all that much, but I sure liked hearing my name roll off his tongue and wondered how it would sound in the throes of passion.

"So, Campbell. I want to be clear, okay? I want to hang out with you. Get to know you. Just, uh, you know? I don't do first date fucks."

I cocked my head to the side, considering his words. He had immediately struck me as someone special, a greater effort to be sure, but watching him as he scrutinized me and asked for more than the regular hook-up had me confused. I'd wanted him for more than random sex to begin with. I hoped he didn't think a quick fuck was all I was good for. I'd lied to him to increase my worth because he was so much more than me. Being with Stone would mean I meant something too. Strange logic, and I couldn't even blame it on the alcohol, because I hadn't had any. I licked my suddenly dry lips and watched Stone's eyes grow wider. "I'd like that too," I finally said, but my voice was so soft, I wasn't sure he'd heard me at first.

Then his face broke out into a full-fledged smile, making him beam like the boy next door, wholesome and vibrant. "So, if I invite you back to my place, you're not going to assume it's for sex?"

I just shook my head; not sure words would actually come out of my mouth at that point. My cock still pressed against my zipper, and I wanted him like nothing else, but he would be so worth waiting for.

"Come on." He nodded to the front door and stood to leave, not looking back to see if I followed. He dumped his cup in the trash, and then as he pushed open the glass door, he stopped and held it open for me.

On the street, an unexpected shyness or self-consciousness crept over me—so not the image I wanted to show. Stone probably wondered where the cocky bastard, who'd walked up and commanded his attention, went. Maybe, I'd left that Campbell back in the club, or he had slowly been discarded piece by piece at Coffee Kraze.

Stone grabbed my hand to get my attention and then pulled me down a side street. Afterward, he kept holding it and I didn't pull away, either. I liked his big hand clasping mine and I really didn't want to let him go. We walked for a while then cut back to the main street headed down 19th toward the railroad tracks. After a few minutes, Stone pulled me down yet another side street and that's when the rain started.

"Oh shit," I said, holding up my free hand.

Stone laughed and tugged my arm. "Come on then."

The quicker we ran, the harder the rain came down. With a loud rumble of thunder, it really broke loose. Stone kept laughing and I followed as close as I could, gripping his hand tight. Part of me wanted to panic, but how could I not join in his delight? Running down the street in the pouring rain hand in hand with a cute boy was sheer freedom—bliss.

We crossed a parking lot and then down 20th and across the railroad tracks. I was about to ask where the hell he lived when he stopped in front of a small complex with some of the apartments above street level businesses. Stone led me to a black iron gate that opened to an interior courtyard and then around the corner and up an outside set of stairs to a third floor unit. It had a small balcony that wasn't half as nice as the ones on the front side of the street.

By the time he fumbled the key into the door and pushed it open, the rain had completely soaked us, our clothes saturated. I stood in his tiny foyer, dripping wet and shaking. Stone pulled at his hoodie. "Get those wet clothes off." He grabbed at his t-shirt, but yanking at our own clothes quickly turned to stripping each other. Stone kicked off his beat up vans, but I'd worn my Union Jack Chucks and had to bend over to untie them. After I kicked them off, Stone helped me peel off my wet jeans, and I noticed he had already pulled his pants off. He stood in front of me in a pair of American Eagle briefs that showed just how happy helping me made him.

He shoved me back against the front door and hiked my foot up, slowly taking off my wet socks, one at a time. Something about the way he pulled them off made the act erotic, and my cock hardened in my still semi-wet 2Xist briefs. They were my favorite neon green pair that barely covered all of me, but didn't show so much under my tight club pants.

We stood there mostly naked and wet, looking at each other. I tried to keep my eyes on Stone's face, and not his wide chest or worse, his hard cock. A drop of rain trickled out of his hair and down his forehead and I leaned forward and licked it before it could travel farther or he could wipe it. I don't know what possessed me to do it, but I needed a taste.

Stone shoved me back playfully. "Hey, I still don't want to have sex tonight."

I couldn't be hurt and wouldn't dare show him if I were. He called the shots. "Yep. I was thinking snacks and Xbox. Right? You play Call of Duty?" I stretched up to look over his shoulder to try and see the rest of his apartment.

Stone scratched at his wet hair. "Yeah, sure. Come on." His words seemed calm and positive, but his eyes looked disappointed. I couldn't help think he expected or wanted me to call his bluff. I didn't want to play games with him, at least not head games. I had enjoyed the physical games, so far, even if they stayed on the innocent side of the line.

"Hey!" I grabbed his arm, spinning him to face me. His skin radiated heat under my cold hands. "Look, Stone. Don't misunderstand me. I want you. Damn!" I eyed him from head to toe, taking in those gorgeous thighs with their smattering of dark hair on golden skin and his shapely calves. "I *really* want you. But, uh, you know. You're worth it. Worth the wait."

In an instant, Stone jumped all in my personal space, his eyes less than an inch from mine with blown out pupils. He made a noise deep in his throat that sounded like a wild animal growling, and it went straight to my gut and made my cock twitch.

"Stone," I gasped.

His warm lips skimmed across mine and his strong arms circled around my back. I stepped into the kiss, opening my mouth and wrapping my arms around his neck. His tongue slipped between my lips to brush against my own. The next moaning sound came from me. The way he held me tight, kissing me like he'd never get another sip, my hips thrust against him of their own accord and I wonder if he would break his own rule. But, no. He pulled away from me, gently, still gazing in my eyes.

I couldn't help the little flicker at the side of my mouth, like a half smile trying to escape.

"Fuck, Campbell. You don't play nice."

"I haven't started playing yet, Stone." As he shoved me, my smile broke free, infecting my face.

"Damn. Come on." He grabbed my hand and pulled me farther into his apartment. The little room in the front held the necessities: a couch, flat screen, and gaming console without much space to spare. Some sports shit hung on the big wall that stretched around to his kitchen area, which wasn't much more than a small counter, stove, fridge, and a sink with only a single bowl.

He pushed me down on his couch and pulled a crochet afghan over me. "You feel cold, Campbell."

I liked that he refused to shorten my name, making everything more serious. Every second I spent with him had me wanting to be closer; I wanted something more with him than I'd ever thought of having. Maybe even that R-word—relationship. Yes, he was absolutely worth it.

2 Stone

Campbell Fain had to be the most incredible man I'd ever laid eyes on. I'd known I was gay at sixteen when I first noticed myself checking out the guys who were checking out the chicks. Damn, none of them had looked like Campbell.

His bleached blond hair, piercings, and even that little peek of tattoo that had played hide and seek with his collar as he moved made him out to be a bad boy but his face was simply angelic; *I swear to God.* His wide eyes begged for attention and his lips, the bottom thick and pouty but the top thin and expressive, called to me like a siren for a kiss. I'd heard other men described as having a strong nose, but that had usually made me think big; Campbell had a straight, strong nose, just the perfect size for his face, sitting nicely between prominent cheekbones. His jaw, lined with dark scruff, was what I could only describe as rugged. The only part of him that looked like his father at all was that little dimple in his chin. He seemed to be clueless of his stark beauty, or perhaps he'd done all of that rebellious stuff to try to hide it. It didn't work.

I couldn't keep my eyes off him in the club as he moved those hips, and when he'd walked over to me, I couldn't believe it. But sitting at Coffee Kraze and talking...just talking with him, became the highlight of the evening.

Campbell appeared so genuine and sweet, despite having grown up in a wealthy home with a very successful and somewhat famous father, Mitchell Fain. His father could be seen all over town on television, radio and billboards as Tampa's premiere personal injury attorney. Yet, Campbell was composed, at ease with himself, especially when he relaxed and smiled, those coppery brown eyes lighting up.

Even beyond all that, I'd had fun with Campbell. We'd run laughing through the rain; Campbell didn't complain once. My heart had pumped harder, and I was unsure if it was the effort of running or simply wanting to get closer to Campbell that had it bursting from my chest.

I knew it was way too soon to say I loved him, but damn the man had me falling hard and fast, and I never did that. I'd had a few hookups; hell, I knew I had a desirable body, but they never lasted beyond a few dates.

Standing in my apartment, dripping wet, I'd wanted to get my hands all over him, but I'd already told him we wouldn't be having sex. I couldn't tempt myself like that. We'd quickly stripped off our clothes. I should have known better, especially when he'd licked at my forehead. It'd been weird and sexy and made me want to drag him to bed. Instead, I'd wrapped him up in an afghan my mother had made for me years before and tucked him into the couch. "Start up the game, if you want. I'll be right back."

I'd finally gotten a good look at that tattoo and found the other on his ribs, too. His chest and collar bone sported a blue rose with a black star under it, and his ribs were covered with writing, but I didn't know what it said. I hoped to find out, up close.

I dashed to my room, partly to find warmer clothes, and partly to hide. It would be easier to get through the night with warm, dry clothes. I pulled on sweatpants and a soft, faded Nike t-shirt. Then I found a pair for Campbell and another t-shirt. The thought of him wearing my clothes made my dick come right back to life after I had just convinced it to go to sleep. The traitorous thing would make being beside him a little torturous, but with Campbell, riding the edge would be oh, so sweet.

Dropping the clothes in his lap, I pointed to the

bathroom. "You'll be warmer once you change."

"Thanks, man." He dropped the afghan on the couch, giving me a bold look at his body as he moved through my apartment. His arms and legs were long and lanky and pale. His chest was smaller than mine, but firm and his stomach was firm as well. When he turned, I watched his totally grab-worthy ass move in that tight green underwear, his cheeks round and mouthwatering. I wanted to nuzzle my nose against that ass.

I leaned back into the couch and waited for him. He'd managed to get the game set up. My system was decent with a thirty-two-inch flat screen that my dad had given me for my twenty-first birthday. So, at least it was relatively new and I didn't have to be embarrassed by it.

The door to the bathroom opened and Campbell came striding across the floor with a smirk on his face, like he figured I'd been sitting in here thinking about his hot body. I'm sure my face looked guilty, but Campbell seemed to like that. He slid onto the couch like a slinky cat, and pressed his leg up against mine, all sinuous and rangy. Next to my bulking thigh, he looked almost delicate. His muscles were defined, but he had zero bulk. "Hey," he said demurely.

"Hey, back." I wanted to tell him how much it turned me on to see him wearing my old Armwood High School t-shirt.

"This where you went to school?" He plucked at the shirt. I wanted to rip it off of him to get at that creamy skin beneath it, wanted to trace his tattoos with my tongue.

"Yeah. They've always had the best football program in the area."

"You played?" He lifted that sexy as fuck eyebrow at me. How did he do that anyway?

I laughed nervously. "Uh, yeah. Quarterback."

"Hmm...that's a new one." He bumped me with his shoulder and picked up the game controller, turning on the game.

"What do you mean?"

"Football players have always been more likely to beat me up than go out with me."

"I'm not just any football player." I nudged him with my thigh and picked up my own controller.

Campbell mumbled, "You can say that again." But I'd heard him loud and clear.

I swallowed hard. "Hey, want a drink?"

He shook his head, calling attention to that still damp shock of blond. It stood on end, all fluffed out, as if he'd dried it with a towel. I forced myself to focus on the game instead, or I'd never get through the night.

Eventually, I broke out the Cheetos and Root beer and we heated up a plate of nachos in the microwave. Campbell fed me cheese covered chips while I decimated a level where he'd already been killed. He sucked at Call of Duty, but I didn't really care about that. My player ended up dying too, because I concentrated on his fingers in my mouth instead of the game. I dropped the controller to the floor and attacked him, pushing his shoulders down against the seat of the couch.

Campbell held the plate of nachos out. "Hey, man! Watch it."

I took the plate and slid it across the coffee table with a little growl. "I can't take it anymore." I leaned over, pressing our chests together. My face hovered inches from him. I took just a moment stare in his eyes. I'd meant what I said; I really couldn't take it anymore. I kissed him hard, sliding my tongue across his lips.

Campbell moaned softly and opened his mouth for me. The velvety brush of our tongues made me tremble a little. Campbell's body writhed beneath me. His hard cock pushing into my hip made me want to shove my hands down the front of his sweatpants. I pushed the thought away and leaned back, reluctantly breaking the hottest kiss I could ever remember having.

"What?" His eyes glassed over with lust.

I didn't want it to end or go too fast. In fact, I needed to savor every second of it. "Still no sex on the first date?"

Campbell turned his head a second, then looked me right in the eye. "Well," he said, looking smug. "It's after twelve and we went from the club to coffee to here, so technically, this is our third date."

I couldn't help laughing at his reasoning.

"That's logical," he said, defending himself; his voice like a purring cat. He rolled his hips, pushing against me, as if to emphasize his point.

"Third?" I shook my head and held back an eye roll. "Maybe, second."

"Don't forget our romp through the rain. You've already seen me practically naked." He wiggled his eyebrows, making me laugh harder.

I leaned in and kissed him again, worried that I wouldn't be able to resist him. When I broke the kiss this time, I stared down at his perfect face. I couldn't stop my hand from trailing across his forehead and resting by his ear, my thumb gently caressing over a cheek bone. My thumb then slid down his face, as if it had a mind of its own, rasping against his stubble and slipping between Campbell's lips. Easily opening his mouth with a little pressure, my index finger touched his tongue, needing to feel such a vulnerable and eager place. It seemed decadent to have my fingers in his mouth. He sucked a bit, wrapping those fabulous lips around me, suggestively, making me want them around my cock. Soon.

I pulled my fingers back out and gazed down at him, taking in his light skin against dark eyes. His brows, lashes, and barely there beard contrasted darkly against pale skin, and his obviously bleached, blond hair slid down over his forehead, not quite hiding the excitement in his eyes. "Beautiful," I muttered before I even realized I meant to speak and pushed his hair back. I was completely enamored with this dazzling young man below me.

Campbell's face lit up with a glorious smile. "You're not bad yourself."

Pouncing on his mouth, this time I simultaneously slid a hand along his side, pushing the sweat pants down. Campbell shoved mine down to my thighs. I barely noticed we'd both gone commando, until our hard cocks bumped against each other. We both moaned in unison.

Straddling his thighs, I pushed up on my knees and took our cocks in hand, squeezing them together gently. "Hold still," I gently commanded him. More than willing to obey, Campbell stilled his movements with a gentle sigh.

I slowly ground my cock between his and the palm of my hand. The feel of rubbing against the silky skin of his hard shaft sent tingles through my dick, convincing me it wouldn't last long. A strangled noise escaped my throat.

Campbell gasped, his pretty lips parting with his sharp intake of breath. Watching his pleasure pushed me over the edge like a hormonal teenager, and I came all over him with a grunt.

Campbell shifted, realizing what I'd done. "No. I'm not done with you," I said, stopping his efforts. I leaned over him and grabbed his cock in one hand, balls in the other. I slid my fingers around in my own cum, using it as a lubricant against his hot skin. Campbell fell back against the couch, his eyes crinkling up and his pink tongue darting out across his bottom lip. "Open your eyes, Campbell." I had to watch his ecstasy.

Slowly, he showed me what I needed, opening his eyes sluggishly. I leaned closer to see they had shifted to a darker shade, and a dark, almost black line circled the outside of the color. His pupils were huge. I thought I saw curiosity along with the lust in them. The thought had my lip lifting at the corner in a smirk. I satisfied the questions in his eyes by gripping his cock harder and twisting with an upstroke. My thumb flicked across the tip of his dick once, twice. His eyes rolled back in his head and his face tightened as cum exploded from his cock, joining mine in a comingling mess of passion.

Campbell looked down and immediately laughed, infectiously, so I joined him. I burst out, "That doesn't count as sex!" That got him laughing even harder, making my heart lurch at the joyous sound.

Could this thing between us be the beginning of something that I'd never had before and might not ever have again? I decided in that moment, slick with our cum and rolling in laughter and watching his bright eyes flashing, that I needed to hold on to this new and fragile relationship with every drop of blood surging through my veins, every solid bone, and every malleable muscle.

3 Campbell

I woke with sunshine streaming into the room and Stone's hot body wrapped around me. His arms and legs and chest had me trapped, but I didn't really want to go anywhere. I snuggled my nose into the crook of his neck. He smelled like sweat and cheese and sex. Oddly, I liked it because underneath I could smell a gentler scent that had to be all Stone.

My eyes closed and my mouth smiled—content. I'd have never guessed this tough, quiet man could be so gentle, sweet...passionate. It wasn't even romance; his slow moves were erotic as hell. He had me needing to come by just looking at me and touching my face.

The buzz of a cell phone on the coffee table had Stone shifting around too soon. He grunted and pulled me tighter. "Shh," he whispered.

I tried not to giggle. Maybe Stone had some kind of control issue, between the way he held me, bossed me around a bit, and stuck to his rules even though I knew he really wanted me. It didn't matter to me though, I sort of found it hilarious, yet I would do anything he said. My chest shook with the force of holding in the laughter. I already loved how much I laughed around him. His presence had me eating at a slice of happiness that I'd never really had before, a new flavor to gorge on. I'd never feasted on this much joy all at once.

Stone growled and sat up. Between the buzzing phone and my barely contained laugh, he had no choice. "Good morning," I said with an escaping giggle.

"What are you laughing about?" He grabbed my arm, pulling me toward him. His arm went around my ribs, and in a flash I slid into his lap, and he tickled me. I shoved at his chest and grabbed at his hands. Stone flipped me over to the floor, wrapping his legs around mine and biting at my neck, and scratching at my skin with his morning stubble.

I wiggled beneath him, laughing so hard I couldn't breathe. "St…Sto…St…" I stuttered through the laughing.

"What? Stop? You want me to stop? This?" He pinned one of my arms over my head and went for my pit.

I screamed, high pitched and desperate.

Stone laughed, but finally let me up.

"You bastard," I laughed out breathlessly.

Stone's grin said he was more than pleased with himself. The gold flecks in his eyes flashed in the sunlight, the green behind them paled. "Good morning, sunshine."

I tried to catch my breath. Everything about Stone shown bright and happy. I didn't want to leave his side. Ever.

"Coffee?"

"Sure. What time is it?" I looked around for a wall clock, but didn't find one. Nothing but sports shit hung on his walls.

He grabbed the offending cell from the table. "Wow. Ten."

We took a moment to stare at each other. Concern flipped over his face, followed by a questioning look. I thought I already knew what he wanted to ask, so like ripping off a Band-Aid, I answered, "I have to go soon."

He nodded, his face dropping into something a lot closer to sadness and I didn't like that look at all. "Not yet. Let's get coffee and maybe a shower first." The corner of his mouth turned up and his eyes were on me again, this time asking for more.

I couldn't refuse him if I'd wanted to. Excitement had my insides jumping, but I played it cool. My over exuberance could scare him off. I crossed my arms over my chest and leaned against the counter, quietly watching him fix our coffee.

We drank it on his little balcony, leaning against the black, wrought iron railing. He spiked his with cinnamon again and it smelled great. A cool breeze made the early morning relaxing and not just bearable in the Florida heat. The sky had already shed its pale gray morning light and loomed above us bright and blue. Mocking birds chattered at everything and nothing in the courtyard. The light mood we'd had moments before had morphed into something quieter and a little more serious, but still delicious and utterly perfect.

I sipped my coffee, grimacing a little at the bitterness. I had to drink it black since Stone was out of milk and sugar. I didn't complain, though. How could I? Even black coffee was perfect with Stone gazing at me as if he could put down his mug and drink me instead.

Somewhere a car door shut and distant voices floated in the air, but we couldn't tell what was said. It was just Sunday morning movement.

"I don't want you to go," Stone blurted out.

My heart skipped a beat, jumping out of sync and into a heavy pounding against my chest. He wanted me. That thought made me unexpectedly happy, and I didn't want to ever leave him. "I don't either. We've still got some time."

"Why are you so happy?"

For once, I opted for the truth. "You don't want me to go." Simple fact.

Stone leaned over and set his mug on the ground then took mine and did the same with it before pulling me into his arms, enveloping me in his heat. "We'll get showered, get something to eat. How're you getting home?"

I shrugged. "Guess I'll call Jay-Jay. I rode with him last night."

"Nah, I'll take you home. But, Campbell...this isn't over." He pulled back and stared into my eyes.

"Good," I answered before he kissed my forehead.

Stone made grilled cheese sandwiches while I showered. I didn't stay in the bathroom long once I realized he wasn't going to join me. I texted Julien to let him know I was alive.

Then we ate the best grilled cheese sandwiches I'd ever tasted before making our way down to Stone's car.

"I'd stay longer, but I have dinner at my parents. They don't like it when I don't show and that just makes everything harder. I'd rather suffer the two hours at dinner than get bitched out all week." True. I didn't need to lie about that, but the intense look on Stone's face made me regret my little white lies from the night before. He scrutinized me as if he could see into my soul and I wanted him to like what he found there. My chest fluttered inside. I knew Stone would turn out to be special, but I didn't realize just how great he really was. I liked everything about him and I swallowed hard, knowing that the lies could easily come back to haunt me. How could I have known he'd turn out to be so perfect?

I wanted to come clean right then but Stone looked at me like no one else ever had, like I was something. Something important—special. I didn't want that to change and it would once he knew I'd lied. I frowned and got in the car.

Stone drove an older, but well taken care of Honda Hatchback. The old silver machine had two dinged up doors and an old and peeling USF sticker gracing the back bumper. Otherwise, it was immaculate. The clean interior was gray and black and the seats were concealed and protected beneath blue covers. "You could probably trick this car out, you know? Get it painted neon green or something."

"Not my style," he said with a slight head shake. No, it wasn't. I liked that. "What do you drive?"

I cringed a little, not wanting to tell him about my flashy car, but I couldn't really say why. "My dad bought me a Beemer last year. I don't drive it much."

"Shit? Really? I'd be driving it all the damn time. BMW. What kind?"

"Just a 320i. Stupid sedan. Respectable. Hell, your car's more fun."

We pulled to a stop at the edge of Stone's complex. "Where we going?"

"I'm on the other side of Tampa, dude. Off Bayshore." I

nodded to the West and fidgeted in my seat. I didn't want Stone to come over. I didn't want him to see where I lived or meet my roommates. I wanted to remain this perfect, beautiful creature he thought I was, unspoiled by the real world.

"Okay." He pulled out of the drive and headed toward Tampa. "You're interesting, Campbell. You'd rather have a crappy Honda than a BMW? Doesn't matter that it's a sedan. Sheesh."

I shrugged. "My daddy bought it. It's the car he wanted me to have. I hate it."

"Wow. That sounds ungrateful."

Maybe I was ungrateful. Stone and I were from different worlds. I'd been given a lot that he'd had to earn and what did I do with it? I resented it. I quit school and got a crappy job that I knew my dad would hate. I didn't work in a law office and I didn't attend school like I'd told him. I had shoved those things in my dad's face. Then when I met someone I wanted to impress, I pulled the possibility out like a calling card and flashed it in Stone's face. None of it was true. None of it was me. I hated the car. I hated that my dad wanted me to be a lawyer, but I'd taken criminal justice classes during my Associate's degree and I enjoyed them, and I hated that I'd enjoyed them. I enjoyed my art history classes a hell of a lot more.

"Hey," I finally said. "I don't really have my life figured out any more than you do. Sometimes it isn't easier just because things are given to you. I don't think I've ever really had to earn anything myself. It doesn't really feel good." I bit my lip hoping he'd understand, but not sure he could.

"I didn't mean—"

"You did. And it's true. Don't worry about it." I stared out the window watching the high rises pass by as we drove through the city. I didn't want to face him. My heart sank into the pit of my stomach. We were already over. As much fun as we had, as much perfection as Stone could potentially be, I still couldn't do it. I couldn't help being relieved that we didn't actually have real sex, since that emotional connection would have been way too intimate—maybe too intimate to walk away from. I hated my decision, hated myself, but I couldn't let anything continue between us. We were too different and I'd never find the strength to keep him.

I gave him directions to the house I shared with Julien and two other guys that went to UT. My dad owned the place, so rent was minimal with four of us. A real steal deal. The large four bedroom with a central living area and gourmet kitchen was located in a neighborhood just off of Bayshore that consisted of mostly older cement block homes, but large ones. My dad knew how to buy real estate. I didn't tell Stone any of that. I didn't even let him pull in the driveway.

He parked at the curb. "This is nice. Can I come in?"

I shook my head. "I don't have time. Maybe later. Look, I gotta go." I opened the door and stuck my legs out of the car door, but before I could get any farther, Stone grabbed my arm, his fingers flexing desperately around my bicep, and pulled me back in toward him. I looked over and saw the devastation in his eyes like he knew I'd already decided to end it.

"Don't. Campbell." His soft voice demanded more from me than what rested on the surface.

He had me caving quickly, but he didn't need me mucking up his life. I wanted him to smile, so I leaned over and kissed him softly. "It's all good, Stone," I lied again.

I got out of the car and walked up to the house before he could say anything else. God only knew what I might say. I wasn't good enough for him. That was the bottom line. Tears stung my eyes as he drove away, but I couldn't let it get to me. I refused.

"Hey, Camp!" Tony called from the kitchen. "Didn't think I'd see you today, dude." He had his nose stuck in a book resting on the counter. He was taking a hard math class at UT and constantly had that heavy text with him.

I swallowed back my hurt—ignored it. "Just stopping in to change before heading over to the 'rents." I rushed to my room before he could grill me further. Julien had already texted that he wouldn't be home until late. His hookup that he'd found at the club had apparently been just as interesting as mine. He'd probably fucked his brains out all day, though. I couldn't seem to get anything right.

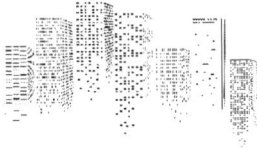

The drive over the bridge to Davis Island didn't take nearly long enough. After finding and loosing Stone so quickly, I couldn't put words to my strung out emotions. The last thing in the world I wanted to do was face my prick of a father.

Guilt at that thought surged in my belly because Stone had been right, and I didn't want to face that either. I had taken everything in my life for granted and I knew damn well that even though my father went about things in a way that never seemed to sit well with me, that he did those things out of love and concern for me.

Yes, he had ambitions for me that I didn't share. Yes, he tended to show his love and support materialistically when I cared so little for material things. Yet, he did still care, and he still included me in his life, even though he probably knew I would never come around. He'd known I was gay for a long time and he had been familiarized with my world view for almost as long. We butted heads on everything, but he was still my father and owed a measure of respect, even though I'd never thought to give it before.

As I pulled into my parent's drive, I vowed I wouldn't call him a dick or any other negative name and stick with Dad or Father. Yep. I could do it; I could play nice.

Glancing up at the old-world style house that had become a familiar fixture in my life, I wondered what it would have been like to grow up in this house. I couldn't remember my parents ever living in a normal suburban neighborhood, but this opulent mini-mansion they'd bought since I'd moved away was simply incredible. Not gaudy or over the top, but every inch screamed luxury from the huge front doors and tiled foyer to the huge kitchen and baths, not to mention the back of the house.

Oh yeah, the back of the house was the show piece, an oasis from the hot Florida sun. They didn't have a pool so much as a cement lagoon. Palm trees circled the manmade pond, gauzy curtains had been tied back across the archways of the covered mezzanine, creating a real Mediterranean feel.

The house itself had huge boxy towers, but the curves around the back, softened that harshness. The Spanish tile roofing and wrought iron railings around the second story balcony helped propagate that old-world feel. And of course, all of that overlooked the bay in spectacular fashion. Stepping out to the back porch at my parent's house might as well have been stepping into another world.

I opened the oversized wooden door and hollered, "Mom!" My voice echoed up the stairs to the second floor where I rarely ventured and through the front room which was supposed to be a family room, yet appeared so formal with antique furniture, Tiffany lamps, and every little knickknack picked out precisely for the spot it sat in. Normally, no one spent much time there unless my parents had a party or something. For a small family dinner, they'd be in the back.

"Camp! In here," my mom called out from the kitchen area. I didn't know why she'd be there, since she never cooked. She had Maria for that, and true to form, Maria stood beside her with busy hands. "Just finishing up. We're eating on the veranda outside." Mom dried her hands on a towel before giving me a hug.

I hugged her back. With my fingers resting on the sliding glass door, ready to open it, I heard her say, "Lorain's here."

Damn it all to hell.

My parents liked to drag our family friend out every so often just to check and make sure I was really gay. After all, Lorain would be a good catch, a lovely girl, and I couldn't argue with that. Someday she'd make a man really happy, but not this man. I wished for the millionth time that she would finally find a guy and settle down so they would stop this nonsense. Knowing my parents, they'd just find someone else, and at least Lorain seemed to be understanding about it all, but I wished she'd stop accepting their invitations.

I braced myself for confrontation and opened the door. As soon as I set foot on the back patio and saw my dad pouring some tropical drink for Lorain, I knew that the only place I really wanted to be was back in Stone's apartment playing video games and fooling around—certainly not standing here listening to my dad chuckle at something clever that Lorain had just said. The surreal moment washed over me, as if I stood in a fragile and fake world. Solid reality waited for me back in Stone's arms.

Lorain tossed her thick dark hair over her shoulder and turned to me with a quick wink. I couldn't argue with her beauty or her charismatic personality, but she just didn't do it for me and neither she nor any other female ever would. Stone on the other hand? Yeah, Stone did it for me alright.

"Camp! Good to see you." At least her lyrical voice gave me something to smile about. She knew she'd been asked here to try to turn me straight. Again. Her complicity didn't make me happy at all. Bitch must have parked in the garage, just so I wouldn't be forewarned.

"Hey, Lulu! What's up?" I used the old nickname that I knew she hated to get a rise out of her.

"Ah, I'm here for dinner." She stood up and offered me a hug. "And don't call me that."

I laughed at the irritated wrinkles above her perfect little upturned nose. We'd known each other so long, she was like a sister to me. I wondered at my parent's audacity. "Good to see you, bug." I hugged her. It was good to see her, and taking out my anger on her wouldn't be fair at all. "It would be nice to see you under some normal circumstances, though."

She laughed, took up her seat at the table and sipped a drink. "Yeah, well, that never happens."

I grunted my response as I shook hands with my father. He handed me a tropical drink afterwards. "New drink?" Dad always played bartender for these afternoon dinners. It seemed to be a fascinating hobby for him, and he tended to make dangerous drinks, mixed really well so you had no idea just how strong they really were. I vowed to only have the one.

"Your mom and Maria put some appetizers together, Son," my dad said in his deep bass. He gestured to the table where weird snack things were set out on a tray. One or two were missing, so I figured they'd been foisted on Lorain already.

"Thanks," I muttered picking up a cracker with some weird gel on top of it. I had no idea what it was, nor did I care. I stuffed it in my mouth and swallowed after barely chewing. It tasted a bit like horseradish and lemon. I ate a second one, hoping that was the requisite number of items required.

Lorain smirked at me, probably because she'd done the same thing.

"So, why aren't you seeing more of this fine young lady, Camp?" I knew it wouldn't take my dad long to drop that bomb.

I closed my eyes and pictured Stone's handsome face. I had quickly become fascinated with his eyes and watching them constantly change colors. I wished I could bring him to this function, but even if we were still together, which I doubted, I could never show up here with him. My parent's would treat him poorly or as if he didn't exist and I couldn't put him through that.

My dad grunted, bringing me back around. "Well?"

"Because I'm gay, Dad." My words seemed more of a bomb than his had. We'd been around this topic so many times.

"Son, don't disrespect your guest."

Disrespect? Was he kidding? They were the ones that summoned her here knowing I was gay. Even Lorain knew. My eyes grew wide and I opened my mouth for some clever yet nasty retort, but Lorain put her hand on my forearm, gently stroking me, like calming a wild animal.

"It's alright, Mr. Fain. I know." She winked at me.

"Lorain, seriously. Why do you keep coming here? This is crazy. I'm never going to date you." I pleaded with her, but she just smiled.

"I'm your friend, Camp," she said with a sigh, leaning back in her chair. After taking another sip of her cocktail, she continued. "I'm not expecting you to date me, regardless of your parent's intentions. Sorry, Mr. Fain. I know you're gay, Camp, and I'm not trying to change you. I'm here to support you."

I shook my head in disbelief. I knew she was my friend and supported me, but I'd never heard her voice that in front of my parents. My dad chose to ignore it, though. That, at least, was normal.

My mom and Maria came out side with plates fixed for the four of us, interrupting anything else that might have been said. The meal tasted wonderful, as I expected with Maria in the kitchen. I guessed the appetizers were my mother's doing, and Maria conveniently made them disappear as we sat with our plates of roast beef, potatoes and gravy. Though a bit heavy for a Florida summer, I didn't blame Maria. My mom was losing it, but she'd never been completely sane as far as I knew.

A few minutes of silence settled over the table as we ate, because heavy or not, Maria's cooking was superb and the meat had been cooked to perfection, falling apart with just the pressure from my fork.

"So?" My mother just had to interrupt the pleasantness of that preferred silence. "Why don't you take Lorain out on the boat after dinner, dear."

"Uh, no. It's too late in the day for that." I had to shoot that idea down quickly. One boat ride would lead to so much more and I did not want to go down that road, even with Lorain.

"Oh, well. I guess you're right," she said, sweetly. I should have known that sweetness for the deception she'd intended. "Why don't you make plans for next weekend then? Come early and take a picnic with you. That'd be fun."

Lorain's green eyes lit up and her mouth formed an *Oh*. I could see the wheels spinning as she thought about how to get out of it, but I could only think about how much fun it would be if I had Stone instead of Lorain out on my parent's boat.

"That sounds like a great idea," I blurted out. "Maybe I can bring my boyfriend. Do you have someone you'd like to bring?" I directed that last at Lorain, knowing I put her on the spot, but not really caring much. Why not make everyone miserable along with me?

"Boyfriend?" Mom practically screeched once she realized what I'd said. "Oh, no. You have a boyfriend now?"

"Yes, his name is Stone," I said, knowing it was at least semi-true. If I were going to have a boyfriend, it would be him, even though we were already over before we ever really had a chance to see this relationship through.

"What kind of name is Stone?" My eyes widened, surprised my dad acknowledged the conversation at all.

"Stone Medlock. That's his name. He's a PA for some wealthy guy downtown."

My dad practically sneered.

"Look, Dad. You don't have to like him or even know him. He makes me happy and that's all that matters."

Lorain's eyes widened. "You should bring him next week. I'm sure your parents would feel much better once they meet him, Camp." As an attorney on staff at his law firm, Lorain commanded more respect than I did in this conversation. My dad looked down on anything less, including me and any boyfriend I might have.

Her words had me choking and I couldn't fucking breathe. My chest pounded with sudden terror. I had already been sweating, but I could have sworn a gallon just poured off the back of my neck. A full-fledged panic attack sat on my chest, making it impossible to suck in that next breath of air. I couldn't decide the cause. Was this anxiety setting in because Lorain had called me out, or because the thought of bringing someone as special as Stone to my parent's house seemed utterly impossible. Or perhaps it was door number three: the fact that Stone would never want to come and meet my parents anyway after how I'd treated him. Ding-ding-ding...I had a winner.

I put my fork down and hung my head. I couldn't back track. I'd never admit I lied about having a boyfriend and give them one more piece of ammunition to use against me.

"What's wrong dear?" my mother asked, but she had a smirk on her face like she knew everything I'd just been thinking. She'd never really supported or accepted me. Both my parents seemed angry that I hadn't turned out to be their perfect son, and as an only child, that made it worse. For once, I refused to feel guilty about it.

"You know what, Mom? I'm not bringing Stone here to face this bullshit."

"Campbell Montgomery Fain." Mother used my full name. *Oh my God!*

I stood up from the table. Dinner was over for me, and I headed back into the house.

Lorain followed after me, grabbing my arm. I spun around to face her. "What?"

"Don't snarl at me, Camp. I didn't do this."

I ran my hands through my hair and blew out a huge gust of air. "I know. Sorry, bug."

She pointed her elegantly, red-tipped finger at me. "That doesn't cut it anymore. I wasn't kidding earlier. I came here as your friend. Listen for once."

"What?"

"I don't think anyone really cares that you're gay. I don't, for sure. But you make everything harder than it has to be. You know? If you could just try to meet them half way, it'd be better for everyone." She nodded her head to the back patio, where I could see my folks getting into it, and I was positive that I was the topic on the table.

"I'm done feeling guilty about my life." My tone sounded anything but convincing.

"Damn, Campbell. Don't be guilty. But, shit...look at you. If you looked, you know, respectable? Well, maybe—"

"Oh, so because I bleach my hair and have a gauge in my ear?" I tugged at the gauge in my lobe a little to emphasize my point. "How I look? That means something to them?" My voice dripped with my intended sarcasm—she couldn't miss my point.

"Shut up. You know what I mean. And go back to school."

"For law?" I practically snarled.

"For something, anything, baby boy. It doesn't have to be law."

I pulled my arm out of her grasp. I hated fighting with her on top of everything, but she was the good little girl, Lorain Montgomery, who did everything her father told her to and got her law degree and joined the family firm. I had even been named after her father. Our parents had practically arranged our marriage from birth, which happened to be her one obligation that would never happen. I wondered if she resented me for it.

I made a beeline for the door and left her calling after me. I was finished with her conversation as well and ready to go home and talk to someone more aligned with my life, like Julien, or a nice bottle of Jack Daniels. Whichever. Didn't matter much to me.

Sadly, the house was empty when I got home, so I made my way to the Jack. That long conversation left me pretty sloshed by the time Julien finally came in.

"Why are you half-naked on the floor, Camp?"

"Stone doesn't love me," I slurred, not sure if that answered his question, but not concerned about it either, especially when the floor spun around to the left while the ceiling spun to the right.

"Fuck, at least put some clothes on." Apparently, Julien didn't care either.

I sat up slowly and watched him in the kitchen making coffee. I looked down at my attire. I wore a sports jersey that I'd found in the dryer, even knowing it probably belonged to Tony. He wasn't really a jock, but he watched sports a lot. I also had on my Diesel Umbr-Andre briefs with their colorful newsprint-like pattern. They were cute and sexy and didn't go with the jersey, but Mr. Daniels didn't care.

I took another swig right from the bottle and laid back down on the floor with one knee bent, pulling my bare foot in and resting my hand around the half empty bottle.

"Sit up, dumb ass."

I didn't want to listen to Julien.

"Now," he said pulling me up to lean my back against the couch. He deftly took my bottle and put a hot mug in my hand to replace it. The room spun a little more, but I knew better than to focus on that. I tried to sip the coffee he gave me, but almost missing my mouth sent me into a fit of giggles.

"Camp, sweetie. I haven't seen you like this in a long time. Come on. What gives?" He nudged me a little and my coffee sloshed, but I stopped giggling and took a sizeable gulp. "Spill it, Camp."

"The coffee?" I asked. With another round of giggles, though this time those little bubbles were more subdued and less self-satisfying.

Julien was not amused. "Listen, sweetie. You need to talk about this or I'm calling your parents to send you to rehab."

We really did need to talk about it, but I didn't want to face anything. "I hate them. Mitchell and Diane Fain," I sneered.

Julien put his arm around me. "What now?"

"Lorain was there again."

For a moment we didn't say anything. He knew the implications of that. Hell, he knew Lorain. "It's not her fault, you know."

I did know, but that's not what I wanted to hear from my best friend. "She's not Stone."

"Who's Stone?"

"The guy. The hookup from the other night. I want him."

"So?"

I shook my head and handed Julien my coffee cup. "I fucked it all up already." I rested my forehead on my crossed arms against my knees. I didn't want Julien to see my face, to see me pouting like a girl, but I was so fucked up.

"What now?" Julien sounded exasperated. He'd been through crap like this with me before. Maybe he didn't understand just how special Stone had become to me already, but he'd certainly heard my tales of woe and misery because I was Campbell Fain. I fucked everything up; that's what I lived for.

"I lied to him about my job."

"What'd you say?"

"That I worked for my dad's firm and I was in law school."

Julien stood up. "I don't get you, Camp. You could fuck up a three-dollar bill."

I looked up at him. "What the hell does that mean?"

Julien sighed as he paced the floor. "I don't know. But, damn. You won't go work for your dad because you are all too proud and rebellious, then you find a guy you obviously like and you're what? Too embarrassed to be working in the file room at Apex?"

"I know, right. It's fucked up."

"Okay. Well, if you like him, really like him, just tell him the truth and start over."

I put my head back down, unable to watch Julien pace. He made the room spin and he had that judging look on his face. "He's special and he's going to hate," I slurred. "Everyone hates me."

"You know what? You're drunk. Go to bed and we'll talk about it tomorrow."

Julien tugged me off the floor and pushed me into my room. I wanted him to stay with me and hold my hand like he'd done so many times before, but I couldn't bring myself to ask him. It was time to grow up and I knew that, even if I didn't want to admit it. Julien and Lorain were both right. I needed to get my shit together or I'd never be able to have a boyfriend like Stone that I could take home and be really happy about without all the lies. If I really wanted my parents to respect me and accept me and my imaginary boyfriend, I needed to do more than refrain from calling my old man a dick.

4 Stone

I missed Campbell a lot and it hadn't even been a full twenty-four since I'd seen him. Despite the fact that he ditched me at the curb, I couldn't let things with him go. I didn't have his phone number, but I knew enough to find him.

Forcing myself to wait until nine to call his office kept me frustrated all morning. I didn't have anything to do for Mr. St. James until later in the afternoon, which gave me an odd morning off and I really wanted to spend some of it getting to the bottom of Campbell's speedy exit. When the clock finally tripped over the hour, I dialed the number I'd found online and called the main office of Fain, Montgomery, Forsyth, hoping to catch him.

A musically feminine voice answered the phone on the second ring. "Fain, Montgomery, Forsyth. How may I direct your call?"

"Yes, uh, I'd like to speak with Campbell Fain."

"Campbell?" She sounded confused.

"Yes, uh, Campbell Fain. Please."

The line was quite for a minute and I was ready to question her, when she finally answered. "Uh, sorry, Sir. Campbell is not in and I don't know when he will be back."

"Can I get a better number for him? It's important."

"Uh, no. Sorry, it's against policy. I can call him with a message, though. If that would be all right with you."

"Sure. Yes. Can you please let him know Stone called and

it's important?" She agreed to pass the message on and I gave her my number, hoping to hear back from Campbell quickly. Yet, hours passed and nothing. I convinced myself that Campbell just had a lot to do. Hell, I would be busy all afternoon myself. Campbell was so perfect for me; I could totally wait for him.

Putting Campbell out of my mind bordered on impossible. Despite my afternoon activity and multiple errands to run, I couldn't stop thinking about his sweet face. We'd had some kind of connection and I wanted more, needed to explore it, and I'd thought he wanted the same. So, why hadn't he called me back? Why did he leave me at the curb wondering if I'd ever see him again? I didn't know those answers, but I was damn sure going to find out before I let him just walk away from me. I wouldn't let him hide when I'd just found him.

I got a text from my boss to pick up coffee for his late meeting, so I pulled a U-turn and headed back toward the coffee joint I knew he loved. For after two in the afternoon, customers packed Coffee Kraze, but I had time, so I got in line and waited with nothing else to do but think about Campbell.

Every time I closed my eyes, I could see that blond hair and eyes like the sweet goo between the spirals of a cinnamon roll. I'd never taken on the role of romantic sap, but Campbell had already left a hole in my chest that ached for him. One way or another I would see him again. I didn't believe in love at first sight or fate, but I wanted to—wanted Campbell to be all of that for me.

The line moved forward. I remembered drinking that shitty black coffee on the patio with him. He acted like it was the best he'd ever drank, but I knew better. I had to douse mine with cinnamon just to stand the taste at all. I wondered if he liked the coffee from Coffee Kraze as much as everyone else seemed to.

The line moved forward again, and I thought about bringing him some after I got off work, but I didn't want to come across as stupid or desperate, a too accurate reflection of my feelings. I wanted to give him everything, but I knew it was too soon and I was being overly romantic and a little silly. I also didn't care—at all.

When I finally made my way to the counter, I ordered for my boss only, having already talked myself out of getting anything for Campbell. As I made my way through town, toward my employer's office, I kept thinking about him.

Why did he let people call him Camp? I hated that. Why did he bleach his hair and let it fall over his gorgeous eyes, which I thought were his best feature? They were so big, they almost didn't fit in his head, but they were perfect. If they were smaller, they'd be lost with that nose and cheekbones. Damn, I really had it bad.

I delivered the coffee and set up for the meeting. My boss wanted me to stay and take notes, so I was stuck for another hour, but I couldn't refuse. I sat down with the laptop St. James had me type up the notes with and relaxed as we waited for everyone to arrive. I normally enjoyed this part of my job, because it gave me an interesting peek into business that I wouldn't otherwise get. But at that moment, I wanted to get my ass over to Campbell's house, not wait around playing secretary.

St. James was just about to get the meeting going. He had changed into the Armani suite I'd picked up for him from the cleaners. He looked very professional, and successful. When I'd first started working for him, I'd had a little crush on him. He came across as moody in a sexy way, but he was straight. I would know because I made reservations for him, and once or twice drove his latest conquest home afterward. That type of errand went a long way to breaking my crush. Now, I just respected his business practices and did my job.

The other attendees sat down around the big table when my phone buzzed. St. James shot me a look, but I just nodded and stepped out of the room. I didn't recognize the local number, and I hoped it would be him.

"Hello. Stone Medlock," I answered in case it wasn't Campbell.

"Hey, uh, Stone. It's Campbell. Uh, Campbell Fain."

I couldn't help smiling, even though he sounded so insecure, and unlike the Campbell I'd spent the night with. "Hey, Campbell. You got my message then? I, uh, I miss you."

"Yeah, I did. Me too. I mean I missed you, too."

"When can I see you again?" I cut to the chase. I'd had enough skating around the issue and St. James was waiting for me.

"I don't know. You know. I'm, uh, I'm pretty busy."

"Me too, and I'm still at work. I'll pick up dinner and be over in about an hour or two. How's that?"

"I don't know."

"Well, too bad. I don't have time to argue. See you in a few hours." I hung up before he could say no. I hated how unsure he sounded, but I didn't think he was playing me. I honestly thought he had some other issues going on and I'd help him get over it, because I needed that man in my life. I just had to figure out the right strategy to get Campbell playing my game.

5 Campbell

I sat down hard on the couch. Stone was coming over. Something painful and raw crawled up my throat. What the hell was I going to do? "Jay-Jay!"

"What now?" Julien came out of the bathroom with a towel around his neck and wearing a pair of track pants that he'd cut off at the knees.

"I need your help."

Julien rolled his eyes. "Oh, fuck no. I know that look." He pointed at me while still gripping the towel.

I gave him my most innocent look and held my hands up. "This is important."

Julien had always been the fun one in our relationship. He always got the hottest guys, knew how to get out of any situation, even when half the time he'd gotten us into those situations to begin with. He was just one of those cool as hell guys that everyone wanted to be friends with, and I still had no idea what he saw in me. He sympathized with me and Lorain and the way our families acted, but he also didn't take our bullshit. He sighed, "What?"

"He's coming over with dinner."

"Tonight?"

I nodded.

"I wasn't planning on going out, Camp. I need to call it an early night."

"That's okay. Stay. I want you to meet him. And..."

"And what?"

"Don't tell him about the job thing. Please? Please?" I begged, hands pressed together in front of my face in supplication.

Julien sighed again. He'd been doing that a lot over the last few days. "Fine. But I think this is a bad idea."

"For the record?"

"Yes," he said, tossing his towel at me. "For the fucking record." He grabbed me before I could throw the towel back, and put me in a head lock. "I've always got your back, but you're being stupid."

I shoved him off me. "I know. Just for now. I promise. If this is going to work out, I'll tell him. But later. Please?"

Julien nodded. "Fine. Let me go get dressed. When's he going to be here and what's he bringing to eat?"

I just shrugged and tossed the towel back at him. He took it and went to his room to change. I figured I should shower and change as well. I'd been sweating at work and I wanted to make a good impression.

Once under the hot water, thoughts of Stone invaded my mind. I jacked off just to take that edge off, then let the hot water pour over my shoulders, hoping it would calm me, but even with the orgasm and hot water, I was keyed up. I hadn't been nervous over a guy like this in a long time. I couldn't even remember the last time. I'd gotten into Julien's love 'em and leave 'em mentality and living up to my looks and snarky attitude. Not as bad as Julien, I wouldn't call myself a slut by any means, but I sure as hell wasn't boyfriend material either. At least not before I met Stone.

He expected my tough guy, happy-go-lucky attitude, and I didn't think I could pull it off again, but I could give it a try. It would start with appearance. I combed my hair back, out of my eyes for once, so the darker roots showed. Then I searched through my closet. I had a ton of punked out t-shirts. I pulled out one with a Marilyn Monroe graphic on it and immediately dumped it on the floor. My other choices consisted of a black t-shirt that I'd cut the sleeves off of or a light sweater that I hadn't worn in three years and might have been a bit faded and gray.

I went with the sweater. It fit a bit tight on me, across the chest, but it made it a little sexier than I had thought, so I kept it. I pulled on my black Seven jeans, because they fit my ass pretty well, even if they were girl's jeans. I didn't know if I needed to wear shoes, but I pulled on my old black Chucks anyway.

I looked like a Goth, a hot Goth, but I still needed something for the right attitude and my old standby eyeliner wouldn't do it. Instead, I snapped on my leather cuff and pulled on a handful of rubber bracelets in black and pink. That would do—just the right amount of rough and sensitive mixed. I barged into Julien's room to look in the full length mirror. He was the only guy I knew that had one—would his vanity never cease?

He stood behind me, wearing faded, worn denim jeans and a plain black t-shirt. "Dude, you look pretty hot. I like the pink bands." He fingered them as he spoke.

I gave him a worried smile. "Are you sure?"

"Damn, this guy really is important."

I lifted an eyebrow at him, wondering what he thought about it all.

"You don't do this." He waived his hand to indicate my outfit. "This quasi-dressed up shit."

I shrugged. "I like him. A lot. A lot-a lot."

"Okay. I get it." He grabbed my shoulders and shook me gently. "I'll be on my best behavior. Come on."

By the time the doorbell chimed, I'd paced a path in the carpet between the kitchen and the living room. Julien had retreated to his room so I bounced to the front door, jerking it open with a wide stance. Stone stood there with bags in his hands and a sexy as fuck look on his face like he'd rather eat me than whatever food he brought. Before I could even invite him in, he took a step forward, invading my space. He leaned into me, smelling my neck and shoulder with a huff that turned me on.

"Can I put these down?" he finally asked.

"Oh, sure. Here." I directed him into the kitchen and he set the bags on the counter and then he was in my face again with his big hand on my cheek and those color-shifting eyes, looking a lot greener with golden specks, staring into mine. He brushed his thumb over my bottom lip, and I opened my mouth slightly. He pushed his thumb in, rubbing it along my tongue for a minute before adding his own tongue and his lips to mine.

"Hey!" Julien's voice interrupted and we broke the kiss, but my eyes didn't leave Stone's face.

"Stone. This is Julien Plant." I nodded to my longtime friend. "Stone Medlock."

Stone took a second before looking to Julien. "Plant? Like the Tampa Plant?"

Julien huffed. He always got that question and it made me wonder why he insisted in living in Tampa if he hated it so much. "Yes, *the* Plant. Nice to meet you." His voice was a bit cold, but tinged with humor. I had to look at him to see if Stone had really upset him, but I didn't want to pry my eyes away from Stone. "He was like my great-great-great uncle or some shit. I'm not a direct descendant but I have the name."

He referred to Henry Plant who had done a lot to establish Tampa and the surrounding areas, including building railroads, the river walk, and a huge opulent hotel that the University of Tampa now owned. The locals and history buffs knew all about Henry Plant. Even though well removed from that side of the family, his ancestry had been verified before his birth. Julien's mother had been a little obsessed with that sort of thing, but not Julien, despite the fortune he would inherit.

"Wow, that's pretty cool," Stone said, but he barely glanced at Julien. He focused on me, making me all tingly. I wanted him closer with fingers in my mouth and tongue exploring my skin. With him standing so close, my semi-hard cock grew thicker as we watched each other, and my desire for him multiplied.

"Okay. Nice meeting you. I'm going out." I hardly noticed

as he left. It hadn't been the plan, but I couldn't blame Julien for leaving when we were hardly being sociable.

When I heard the door shut, my knees went weak, knowing we were alone. "I want you in my bed," I said, breathy and wanting.

He stuck his thumb back in my mouth and followed it with his tongue. I had no idea why I found that so sexy, but I did, so I ground my hard cock against his hip, silently begging him for more.

"I came over to talk to you, but all I want to do is claim you. Make you mine."

I sucked on his thumb and watched his eyes grow wide, pupils large and demanding. "Come," I said, tugging his arm to follow me. Fuck the snark, fuck the attitude—I had to have him.

6 Stone

"Tell me you're not just playing me, Campbell. I need to know this is—you know—something. I think this can be something real between us. Am I wrong?" We fell into his bed. The room was dark and cool with a ceiling fan circulating the air, creating an oasis from the Florida heat, but not from the passion burning through my veins as I hovered over him.

Campbell looked up at me with sincerity and want glowing in his serious, brown eyes. "No, my God, no. I wouldn't do that. If this was just a hookup, I'd have said so. Hell, I'd have done something about it and moved on."

I propped myself up on one elbow, almost cradling his head. I had to touch him, the reflex completely out of my control when I looked at him this closely. I slid the pads of my fingers across his lips and when they parted, I couldn't help darting one inside his luscious mouth. He licked at them with total abandon. My cock loved it and wanted that mouth. Those lips totally needed to be on my cock. "We're wearing too many clothes."

We sat up and pulled our shirts off. When I turned back to him, Campbell sat on the edge of the bed, wearing just his jeans with all that creamy skin stretched out above. He had a long waist and two flat brown discs around his nipples. I got a good view of the tattoo on his ribs and ran my fingers across it, feather light. "What's this say?"

Campbell stretched out on his side and lifted his arm so I

could read it. I crawled over him to get closer, as I examined the words.

"You are a free spirit, a rebel child
flowing where the wind blows,
and life will never slow you down;
destiny decides where you go,
eternity will bring you around."

"That's very poetic."

"Yeah. I thought so. My roommate, Gavin, wrote it. He's kind of a poet, creative type." He grumbled softly, "Part of my rebellious phase."

I snorted. "Aren't you still in your rebellious phase?"

Campbell laughed and I thought my heart would burst free of my chest.

I came undone just from the sound of his laughter, and I couldn't get enough. "Well?"

"No. Not really. I'm more in my figuring out life phase," he said, more seriously than before.

"I don't know, Campbell. It seems like you have things figured out to me. You're going to school, going to be a hot shot lawyer, like your dad. I respect that man. You seem to be making great choices. You have your shit together." I couldn't help lean over and kiss him. My fingers made their way to his hair. "I love touching you," I whispered, as we reluctantly broke the kiss.

"I can tell. I like it too."

The want in his eyes had my body humming and the blood rushing to my dick. I shoved his shoulder back against the bed and pressed my bare chest into his, needing skin on skin contact. Wanting more, but not willing to rush the perfection, I cupped the side of his face, and stroked his cheek with my thumb.

His eyes grew dark and challenging. "Kiss me again, please." He asked me so sweetly, I surely could not resist.

I took his mouth with mine and owned it, shoving my tongue in deeply, wanting to mark him on the inside somehow. It wasn't rational, I'd lost rational. My need for him overwhelmed my senses. I fucked his mouth with my tongue and Campbell took it, took all of it. I showed him how turned on I was by grinding my cock against him with the same rhythm I assaulted his mouth.

Campbell moaned around my tongue, as if begging for more. I couldn't resist anything he asked of me. I pulled away from the kiss, replacing my tongue with my index finger. He sucked the digit as I leaned up on my knees and pulled at the button on his jeans with my other hand. "I want you Campbell. I want to take you, fuck you, make you mine."

"Do it," he said when I employed both hands to tug at the tight as fuck denim covering his ass. I pulled the material down to reveal long skinny legs that went on forever. I couldn't wait to have them wrapped around my waist.

I stood up and pulled my pants and underwear off, dropping them on the floor beside Campbell's clothes. My eyes feasted on him, lying before me naked with all that creamy skin, long limbs, and hard pink cock that ended with a purple crown that I had to have my mouth on in the next second or my heart would just stop.

I ran my fingers up his lean thighs with their defined muscles. He had to be either a runner or a swimmer with those long legs, but I could figure that out later. My hands cupped around his hips and my tongue flicked across the head of his cock.

"Oh, God. Stone, more." His words were pure pleasure in my ears, and I could only give in to them. I wrapped my mouth around his cock and took him in slowly, wanting to savor every second of his flavor—like apricots without the sweetness. As I sucked him, my fingers roamed across his hips and flat stomach. My fingers found the little indent in his belly. His chest and stomach were free of hair, and he was very neatly trimmed around his cock. I'd thought I liked guys with hair on their chest, but I found his bareness totally erotic in true cock-pulsing form.

Campbell pulled his legs up, planting his feet on the edge of the mattress. His bare feet were just as lithe as the rest of his body. Part of me wanted to stop and suck on his toes, but that could come later. I enjoyed the little grunts and whines Campbell made as I worked over his hard cock. It didn't have much girth, but it was perfect for him, long and lean and I instantly fell in love with it.

I moved my hand that wasn't fingering his belly button down the back of his thigh and under his balls. They pulled up tight and Campbell's moans got louder. "Do you want me stop?"

"Oh God, no. Sto…one," he groaned dragging my name into multiple syllables. More than happy to oblige, I sucked him harder and faster. I fluttered my fingers behind his balls, feeling them pull even tighter just before he exploded in my mouth. His cum tasted rich and fruity and salty and only slightly bitter. I knew I could easily be addicted to it, to him.

I leaned over him again, watching him slowly release the death grip he had on his comforter. "You okay?"

He shook his head, eyes tightly closed and making wrinkles along his eyelids. "No. Not alright. I need more. Need you. Now."

"Need me how, Campbell?"

He opened his eyes and gazed up at me. He opened his mouth, words didn't come out, but it left a tempting opening and I slid my finger in his mouth again. His eyes fluttered as he wrapped his lips around me.

"I want to fuck you, Campbell. Is that what you want?"

He nodded, but didn't let go of the suction around my index finger.

"Lube? Condom?"

Campbell scrambled out from under me and up to the head of his bed. He leaned over to get the necessities out of his drawer and gave me the perfect view of his sweet ass at the same time. My hands seemed like moths drawn to the light of his body. I'd never been so out of control as I grabbed his ass, his hips, and slid my hands down his thighs. The rest of my body prepared to act; my chest plastered itself against his back and my cock slid along the crease of his ass.

He dropped to the bed, a bottle of lube in one hand and a condom in the other, and his chest pressed into the mattress as I let most of my weight press against him. A loud moan burst into the room, deep and low, and I realized it was mine. "Campbell. You feel so perfect."

"More. Fuck me, Stone."

I knew I needed to get him ready and I wanted to watch him come unglued as I touched him. "Roll over," I said, moving my body off of him, though it didn't want to let him go.

Sitting back on my heels, I shoved my thick thighs under his and pushed his knees apart. His flaccid cock jerked to the side and filled out a bit as I watched him, staring at his beautiful private parts. My eyes scanned up his chest and to his face. He had his arms wrapped behind his head and his dark eyes focused on my face with a slight smirk. "What?"

The smirk spread out to a full smile before he answered me. "I don't think I'll ever get enough of your hands on me."

"Me either." I forced my eyes away from him and opened the lube with a snick. I poured a liberal amount on my fingers. I swear they were tingling just knowing where they were going next. Another claim on this gorgeous man, I slid my sticky fingers along his taint and slowly into his hole. I watched his face morph through several versions from uncomfortable to relaxed and finally to passion as I pumped my fingers in and out.

After a few minutes of stretching and exploring Campbell's most intimate part, I watched his face fly into ecstasy when I hit his prostate. His cock had been more than semi-hard by then, but when I hit that button, it practically leapt off his body, filling out completely, long and hard. As much as I wanted that titillating piece of him, I wanted to be inside him more.

Campbell practically growled at me, his face filling with disappointment when I removed my fingers.

"Getting the condom, tiger." I ripped the package open and rolled it down my cock, quickly, not wanting either of us to wait any longer than absolutely necessary. I poured another handful of lube and stroked my cock, priming it for action.

"Now," Campbell snarled.

"Damn, you're feisty. Shh, little tiger. I got you." I pushed my cock against his hole, rubbing it in small circles while I waited for Campbell's face to go back to that relaxed mode. His eyes fluttered, his lashes dark against his pale cheek, as he calmed. Before he could get frustrated again, I shoved forward with a slow roll of my hips, pushing through his tight ring of muscle. I reveled in the hot grip as his body stretched, taking me in.

Pulling in and out with short jabs, I pushed farther in with each stroke, until pressed fully against him, my balls touching his ass. The heat of him wrapped tight around me. I rubbed up and down the back of his thighs, against the light hair that gave just a bit of friction. "You okay, tiger?"

His eyes opened, slowly and captured me in his arduous gaze. He didn't need words to demand what he wanted, I could see it in his face and I would answer his challenge; my hips snapped forward with considerable force. The rest of the world melted away and I knew only Campbell in front of me begging with his eyes to be fucked hard, and that's exactly what I gave him.

I pulled farther up on my knees, grabbing his thighs and he rested his feet against my shoulders, spreading his knees. My speed ramped up and I slammed into him hard and fast, needing something, anything, just more.

I leaned in and he wrapped his legs around me. Unable to stop myself, I licked and nuzzled his neck, under his ear, licked at that lobe stretched out by his gauge. He had a black gauge in and it wasn't huge like some guys you would see, only about as big as his thumb nail. Silver studs and hoops climbed along the edge of his ear above it.

Each flick of my tongue and thrust of my hips had Campbell making sexy grunts and moans. He ran his hand across the sides of my head, where I kept my hair cut short and then up into the longer curls at the top, and then trickled down the back of my neck. Still I fucked him harder. I looked down at the bliss and need on his face and I wrapped my arms around his thighs so I could pull and push him as we fucked.

"God, Stone," he groaned and grabbed his cock, stroking in time with the rhythm I set. His neck arched and his head tilted back as he grunted again, then his body trembled, legs shaking. "Now! Now!" He came hard, shooting out over his fingers and dripping onto his stomach.

In a wave of lust, I wanted to lick his stomach clean. The thought of such an erotic deed had my balls pulling up tight, and a moment later my eyes flashed with a strange white light as that orgasmic rush surged from the base of my spine and out my cock, filling the condom. I wished we'd been bareback in that moment, wanting nothing more than to release inside him and mark him in one more way as mine.

A moment later, I collapsed down on him with my own grunt. "Damn, you're heavy," Campbell laughed and shoved at me, so I rolled off and onto my back, holding onto the base of the condom as I slid out of him.

"God Campbell, that was..."

He chuckled a little. "For me, too."

I leaned up on my elbow and faced him. I plunged my fingers in his blond hair, and pulled him to me for a kiss, needing some physical reassurance that I wouldn't be kicked to the curb again. His demanding lips answered that without words, kissing me back hard and confident and stable.

7 Campbell

Getting up the next morning was a rush of Stone throwing on his clothes and dashing off because he didn't want to be late to work. We were both up earlier than normal and I struggled to get out of bed, but it went a lot faster when his warm body wasn't in it, heating me up. I sat up when he brought me coffee. "Not sure how you like it, but I added a little cream and sugar. That okay?"

"Fuck yeah," I mumbled back, sipping on the heavenly brew. "You can stay over any time you want if you're gonna bring me coffee."

"Whatever, asshole," he said, trying unsuccessfully to be mad. How could he sound mad with that huge grin on his face, announcing to the world that he just got laid? I supposed mine would look like that all day too. Hell, that man could fuck me into the mattress any time.

After a few quiet moments filled with drinking our coffee and looking at each other, I couldn't take it anymore. "So, you're off then?"

"Yep."

"When, when do you want to, uh?" I barely got the words to leave my tongue.

"Whenever you want. I'm probably working late the next few nights, though." He shrugged, as if his work was an inevitable but necessary evil. Or maybe he thought that it just wouldn't be as fun as spending time with me. I'd like to think a little of both, but I didn't know.

"You have my number now, right. Just call me. Whenever."

Stone's eyes were dark and questioning, but he didn't say anything. His leaned in and kissed me quickly on the lips. I wanted to take it deeper, not knowing when I'd see him again, but I didn't want to subject him to morning breath either. Then he slid his tongue between my lips, obviously not caring. My heart pounded harder as he kissed me.

Watching him walk down my driveway practically cracked me open with its difficulty. Although I knew he wasn't walking away from me, my soul didn't seem to understand that. These two differing contemplations confused me. With a deep sigh, I figured I'd better get ready and get my ass to work instead of worrying about things I couldn't change.

After a quick shower, I dressed and then made my way to the kitchen to make a to-go cup before heading out. Julien leaned against the counter on one arm, eyeing me as if he'd been waiting for me there for hours. "What?"

He made some kind of chuffing noise and rolled his eyes.

"Seriously. What, Jay?"

He stood up and straightened his tie, looking very much like he was choking himself. I certainly didn't envy his office job, wearing a suit, and staring at a computer for hours. Desk jockey material? Not me. "That guy, Stone?" he finally asked, apparently satisfied that his clothes were aligned.

"What about him?"

"I think he could be really good for you and you're a shit for not telling him the truth."

I snorted.

"Fuck you, Camp."

"How do you know I didn't?" I hid behind my coffee cup, not liking where he led the conversation but not mature enough to change it. What next? Calling him names or giving him the *I'm rubber you're glue* speech. Yes, real mature, Fain.

"Because I know you. Don't fuck this up man. Get your shit together already."

I blew out a long breath and spoke so quiet, not even sure he'd hear me. "I'm trying." Yet, I knew I wasn't trying hard enough. I'd let Stone go on about school and my wonderful future that really didn't exist. The guilt of it sat in my heart like lead.

He put his hand on my shoulder for a moment, then left without another word. He'd known me almost my entire life. We'd met at private school in second grade. He stood up for me when three girls had shoved me down in the sandbox on the playground. I'd always been the smallest kid in class and for years the girls towered over me and they were fucking mean. Lorain and Julien had been the only people I could count on to not bully me mercilessly. They quickly became my shield and sword. It seemed like things hadn't changed much in the past fifteen years or so. I had more of an attitude, but still seemed to be in just as much trouble, and they were still trying to help me out of it.

Their lives had changed, though, and I needed to acknowledge that. Lorain and Julien had careers; they had grown up to some extent, more than me anyway. Apparently, I couldn't leave high school—stuck with the same shitty attitude I'd always had. How would I ever manage to keep Stone like that? He'd moved so easily into the relationship, fluid, like diving effortlessly through water, but I kept tripping over cracks and pebbles, unable to make it to the pool. Even without a degree, he had more of a career than I did and obviously more maturity.

Shaking my head, I topped off my coffee and got the hell out of there. I needed to get to work. Even if I didn't have a career like the others had, my job allowed me some freedom that they didn't have. I had less responsibilities at work and didn't run into a lot of forced overtime or stress. I knew I had that much and tried to appreciate it. Working in the mailroom was still my job and I couldn't lose it, so I better not be late.

I parked in the parking garage and walked across the street, making my way through the employee entrance and up to the fifth floor where I punched in. The building had ten floors of glass that looked out over Tampa and part of the Hillsborough River. I enjoyed the views as I made my way through the building with my metal cart, making the daily deliveries.

Apex was a corporation like any other for the most part. I'd heard the gossip and backstabbing that went on, but thankfully, I stayed well removed from the political garbage. The best part of working here was that it was an LBGT friendly organization. I knew they did a lot of fund raising and very public events for the community, including sponsoring a gay motorcycle racer. I didn't follow that before coming on board, but during the racing season, the promotional material showed up everywhere. I could be proud of the company I worked for, but not necessarily my position in it. I knew I could do better, but it took having to tell Stone I was just a mail clerk to make me realize it. Damn. That man turned my world upside down.

Right after lunch my phone buzzed. Part of me hoped to see Stone's number on the screen, but instead I saw my father's law firm. I answered quickly, ducking into an empty cubby. "Yeah," I answered.

"Campbell? It's Kimmy." She worked for my dad as a paralegal.

"Hey, Kimmy. What's up?"

"Your dad would like you to come by the office after work. Can you get here by six?" Late hours were the norm for my dad. He often had to deal with clients that couldn't or wouldn't get to his office until after regular business hours, so no surprise there.

"Sure. Why?"

"Can't really talk about it. Just come and put your big boy pants on before you get here, okay?" She sounded somewhat uncertain and I didn't like that.

"Am I in trouble?"

"Uh, yes and no. Don't put me on the spot. It's not that bad. Okay?"

She'd always tried to look out for me with my dad, though

I never really knew why. "Okay. Thanks, Kim."

"Sure. See ya tonight."

I shoved my phone in my pocket and got back to work, worrying the rest of the day. I never knew what I would face when Dad called me in like that. He hadn't done it in a long time. I guessed he would be dressing me down for treating Lorain poorly and leaving so abruptly from our Sunday dinner, but I wouldn't apologize for any of that. Whatever the dick had to say, it'd better be worth my time.

I spent the next hour pulling my attitude up to my neck and wondering if that would really help me any. When had I started questioning everything?

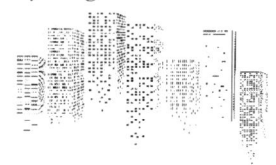

At five to six, I waltzed into my father's front lobby of Fain, Montgomery, Forsyth. I didn't see Kimmy at the front desk, but Dad's secretary was there. "He's not ready yet. Sit." She pointed at the sofa and chairs set up in their lobby.

Granted, the furniture was much more comfortable than my own, but when I had to wait for my father, that didn't account for much. I might as well lie on a bed of nails.

I sat down anyway, grumbling under my breath the whole time. Complaining to his secretary wouldn't do any good. She tended to be stiff, abrupt. I'd rather talk to Kimmy, but didn't want to bother her either, so I just waited, sending off angry vibes that everyone ignored.

After a few minutes, shouting came from the back room, making me stand up instinctively. I moved beside the reception desk and looked down the hall. A man stormed out of my dad's office. He was as tall as me, but with a lot more muscle. I wished I had been to the gym more, because his attitude was threatening. The anger rolled off him like a bowling ball flying toward the pins, and I did not want to be in his way. His reddish brown beard was neatly trimmed and his hair cut in a shaggy, but short-enough style and he wore a suit and tie that strained around his shoulders. His dark eyes flashed with passion and I'm sure I would have been turned on if not for the firm set of his jaw, thin lips pursed tightly together and his eyebrows that threatened to collapse on his nose, they were so pulled in. Yep. He was totally pissed.

I presumed his anger had to do with my father, but he slowed down as he passed me, giving me a hard accusing look before thundering through the front door, the wood slamming in its frame. My jaw dropped open a little thinking about what I'd just seen, but I had no time to reflect. My father called for me. "Camp!" He gestured to the conference room. I thought it odd, since we always met in his office, but I followed him anyway.

"What's going on Dad? Who was that guy?"

"Just an unhappy client. It happens. He didn't want to listen to me, didn't take my advice." He held up his hands, helplessly. "So, he wasn't happy with the results. Don't worry about it, Camp. You're here for another reason." He pointed to a bouquet on the side board.

Tiger Lilies.

I knew who had sent them without even looking at the card, but Dad shoved it in my hand, so I read it quickly.

Campbell, enjoyed our time together. Can't wait to see you again, Tiger! -Stone.

"Wow!"

"So, this is from the new boyfriend? You can't have him sending this here. This is a place of business, Camp."

"Yeah, Dad. Sorry. I'll take care of it. Promise," I responded, still staring at the note. I couldn't believe Stone had done that. I thought I'd nipped the whole where I work thing in the bud by giving him my number. Guess not.

"Seriously, Camp. Can you keep your private life private already?"

I looked up at my dad. He looked almost as pissed as the guy storming out of his office a minute ago. I didn't get it. The note hadn't said thanks for the fuck or anything. "Geez, Dad. I said I'd handle it."

He snorted. He actually snorted. "I don't really trust you to handle anything right about now."

My mouth fell open. I couldn't believe he'd said that to me. I tucked the card in my back pocket and grabbed the Lilies. They were really beautiful. "Sure. Whatever." *Fuck you!* I turned to leave.

"Camp!" he called after me, but I had to ignore him.

Yeah, I thought it was pretty mature of me to walk out instead of telling him off, so I did that with a mental pat on the back.

8 Stone

When Campbell texted me to thank me for the flowers, I could barely contain my joy. I didn't want him to feel girly, but I wanted to let him know I was thinking about him with a small bouquet, nothing over the top. Based on his text, he received it well, leaving me frustrated about working late hours when I really wanted to see him, be with him.

I tapped out a few more notes on my keyboard before St. James came strolling in to the front office. "Stone, man! Get out of here. The rest of that will wait until tomorrow. Hell, what time is it?" He looked at his sleek Movado watch. "Oh, man! It's late. Seriously. Get out of here."

Giving him a quick salute, I closed my laptop. He didn't need to tell me twice. I couldn't keep myself from dialing Campbell's number on the way down to the parking garage. He answered on the third ring. "Hey, Campbell."

"Stone! Just thinking about you, man." His voice put a cheery end to my day and I wanted to hear a lot more of it. I wanted to hear it panting out my name.

"Meet me at Taco Bus on Franklin." I loved that place and not just for the cool old-fashioned school bus that sat in front of the store, but also for the good food and being close to where I worked on Franklin.

"Sure. I'm hungry."

I got there first and picked up a couple of Coronas and a couple of tacos and burritos. I'd only finished one taco before

Campbell came up to the table looking delicious enough for me to forget the Mexican food and eat him.

He wore a white t-shirt with a large red graphic design, that reminded me of the Japanese sun flag, under a light, black jacket. His stark blond bangs hung out of the side of a Tampa Lightning ball cap and his afternoon whiskers appeared dark on his cheek and chin. His black jeans had a hole in one knee, but otherwise hugged his legs as if they were never letting go. Damn, his legs stretched out, long and skinny and made to wrap around my waist, leaving me fighting a hard-on. And maybe drooling—just a little.

"That's not enough food," he grumbled and pulled out a chair, turning it around backwards to straddle it across from me.

I slid a beer over to him, and he took a long drink with a mumbled, "Thanks."

"Order whatever you want, Campbell."

He sat the beer on the table and looked at me with his dark eyes. "I kind of missed you," he said with a quirky little smile that did wicked things to my heart.

After he ordered enough food to feed half of the defensive line for a football team, he dug in. "I'm freakin' starving."

"How the hell do you stay so skinny eating like that?" I watched him shove a burrito in his mouth.

He shrugged one shoulder and swallowed his food. "High metabolism?"

We both laughed a little, before a strange awkward silence fell over us. "I'll get us a couple more Coronas." Just to break the tension, I got up and went to the counter and waited under the giant yellow and black sign.

After much food and another beer, Campbell pushed back away from the table. "Hey, listen, Stone."

"Huh?" Why did I feel like he was already breaking up with me again?

"I totally loved the flowers. Tiger lilies." He smiled with his whole face, showing me just how much he really did love my gift. Then his face drooped. "But you can't send things to my work. Please. I'll get in trouble."

"What? That's stupid."

He sucked his bottom lip in between his teeth. "I know, but my dad. Shit. You know he's weird. He knows I'm gay, but hates to admit it. So, he said I paraded my gay flag all over the office or something. I told you he's kind of a dick. So, it was really nice, but don't." He shoveled another taco in his mouth, as if to shut himself up.

"Okay. I didn't mean to get you in trouble. No problem. I just wanted you to know...you know?"

He drank the final swallow of his beer. "I know."

Our eyes met across the table. His eyes were a bit lighter under the fluorescent lighting, but still expressive and large like a puppy's, and they had a world of want shinning in them. I needed to fulfill that want and satisfy him in every way I could think of. "Let's get out of here."

We walked around to the parking lot in the back of the store and leaned up against my Honda. I had parked it back against the wall of the building, so it sheltered us some from the view of the street. "Where'd you park?" I looked around for Campbell's fancy car.

He slid up against me, wrapping his arms around my waist and snuggling his nose into the crook of my neck. "I didn't. I took a cab. In case we were drinking."

"Smart."

"Whatever." He leaned back so I could see his eye-roll and we laughed.

"No partying tonight, though. We both have to get up and go to work tomorrow."

"Stay with me tonight?"

I blew out a long breath. "I can't. But, damn! You know I want to, Campbell."

He ground his crotch up against mine to try and convince me, and it almost worked. I wanted desperately to touch him, skin to skin. "Hey, come here," I begged and pulled him up to meet me face to face. "I want you." I kissed him, pressing my lips to his. When he opened for me, I slid my tongue inside his mouth, rubbing against his tongue, loving the wet friction.

A little whelp came from him and I wanted to devour him. Our kiss deepened and more crotch-grinding accompanied it. My mouth trailed down his jaw to his neck, I bit and sucked there, while I touched his silky lips with the tips of my fingers. In a slow determined motion, my hands wandered their way down his back and around his waist, then pulled on the button of his jeans.

"What are you doing?" he whispered.

"It's dark, getting late. No one's going to see."

Campbell snickered as I fought to shove those tight jeans off his hips a little to get a better grasp of his long, hard cock.

When I had him where I wanted him and pulled off a few strokes, loving the little cooing sounds he made, he stopped me with his hand on my wrist. "What?"

"Wait." He pulled the button on my fly and shoved my Kakis open, grabbing at me and sliding my briefs down to expose my dick. The cool air blowing over it only made it harder. "I want you too, Stone."

He put one foot on the bumper of my car to lift himself a little to get better leverage, but afraid he would fall, I let go of him and wrapped my hands around his ass, which only pulled him closer, our cocks lining up and brushing together.

"Oh!" he groaned and wrapped an arm around my neck and the other got stuffed between us and he grabbed both of our cocks, rubbing them together as he ground against me. "Fuck! More!"

I couldn't argue with that. My own response was a low growl from deep in my throat that only got louder as Campbell grunted. I wanted to fuck him so badly, but with his skin sliding against mine so tantalizing, I couldn't get enough of just that sensation. The added excitement of getting caught only spurred us on headlong toward our orgasm. "Ahh...fuck, harder, Camp!" My hips rocked forward of their own accord.

"Yes, yes, close. Fuck!"

I could tell from his eyes scrunched up and his face, tinted yellow from the streetlight, he was fighting to come. The intensity overwhelmed me. "Campbell," I moaned out, exploding all over his hand. "Too much! Ah..."

He answered with another grunt and barked out, "Fuck!" as he came with me. His face relaxed and he leaned against my chest, his body warm and firm.

"Damn, Campbell. That was so hot." I held him tighter, not wanting to let him go.

He kissed my neck and jaw. "Yeah, nice," he purred, nibbling at my chin and searching for my lips. He kissed me lazily. "If we were home, I'd so stretch out on the bed. God!"

"Yeah, well, I need to take you home, anyway."

"Not yet. Don't let go."

After a bit more snuggling and a quick clean up using some napkins I had stashed in the glove compartment, I drove Campbell across town to his house.

"Come inside?" Campbell asked as I stopped at the curb.

I shook my head a little and looked down at my hands resting on the bottom of the steering wheel. "I, uh, gotta get up early. Like I said. So, rain check?"

I glanced up, but couldn't see the disappointment on his face through the darkness, though I heard it in his words. "Uh, yeah. I guess so."

"Hey?" I responded quickly. "We have plenty of time. I'm not seeing anyone else. I like you. A lot. You're perfect for me. Not just your looks, but who you are. You're focused and I admire you for going after what you want and going to school to follow after your dad. Plus you are so sweet and sexy. Seriously, let's make plans for this weekend."

"Okay." I could hear the smile returning and leaned in to kiss him. Thankfully, Campbell returned the kiss with tongue and lips and his hands on my face. I wanted to touch him, too and couldn't stop myself from pushing my hands through his hair, knocking his cap off.

"I like that." Campbell closed his eyes and rubbed against my hands like a cat.

"Mmm. Me too. Friday night. Okay, tiger?"

"Sure."

He got out of the car and waved to me as he made his way across the lawn to the house. I watched until he went inside before pulling away from the curb.

I wanted to just say fuck it all and join him. I could be knocking on the door in five seconds and was pretty sure Campbell would open it for me. Morning would come too early, though, and I didn't want to rush things. I wanted something more than fucking and fun. Campbell was worth so much more than that, and I vowed to give him the best date ever on Friday.

On the way home, I thought about Campbell. This new relationship dazed me, just how much I wanted Campbell in my life sort of bowled me over. No other person had ever had my emotions running so hot before. I had to admit I'd been wanting more of a relationship with someone for some time. In those lonely moments of the day, how could I not want someone to share my life with? So, was I in love with being in love or in love with Campbell?

Most guys I'd met up to this point had never really wanted a relationship, or at least a monogamous one, so my experience with real relationships was nil. I wanted more, but I also wanted it with Campbell. Friday night I was going to ask him for a boyfriend type, committed relationship and the thought scared the crap out of me, because Campbell could very well say no. I really hoped he wouldn't, hoped he was different. I needed the reality of a relationship with Campbell to live up to my expectations.

When I got home, I needed to distract myself from worrying about him, so I signed on to my Xbox and slid my headset on. I found a few guys I played with regularly and got a game going. After a lot of yelling and cursing and clowning around, I decided I'd better get to bed and signed off.

They were a fun group, but playing with them wasn't nearly as fun as it had been playing with Campbell. Admittedly, Campbell wasn't very good, but watching the excitement on his face after a great move or a good shot had made my heart thump hard. The way he had stuck his tongue out of the corner of his mouth when he concentrated had made my cock hard. I hoped we'd have some Xbox time over the weekend.

By the time I finally crawled between my cool sheets, I couldn't get Campbell's face off my mind. So much for using gaming to distract me. My cock slapped against my stomach, harder than ever and I really wished I'd followed Campbell across his lawn and into his bed.

I wanted him in my bed Friday for sure. I imagined what I'd do with him, spreading his legs and licking his hole. I'd never done anything like that before, but wanted to with him. I wanted to explore every inch of his lithe body with my hands and mouth. I shoved my briefs down my thighs and stroked my cock, long and slow.

More images of Campbell's face crossed my thoughts, I imagined the look of ecstasy on his face as I touched him and pleasured him. I jacked my cock furiously, hoping for a quick release so I could sleep. Grabbing my balls with my other hand, I thought about sliding my cock inside him and pictured his face with those expressive, dark eyes growing wide when I did it.

His mouth would fall open and I'd lick along his strong jaw line as I pumped into him. I wanted to push his legs up around his ears and plow into him hard until I couldn't breathe and Campbell shot out hot, sticky cum between us. The thought had me coming hard, squirting on my chest and over my fist. I grabbed a dirty t-shirt off of the floor and wiped up before rolling over and enjoying that little piece of nirvana found only after a good orgasm. With a sigh, I closed my eyes and drifted off to sleep.

9 Campbell

I'd had such a good time with Stone and hated waking up in a cold bed without him. I'd tried several times to set the lies straight, but I choked. Every time. I couldn't do it. *When he finds out, he's going to hate me and I just can't stand the thought of seeing disappointment in his eyes.* I wanted Stone to look at me like I was the only thing in his world worth looking at. I wanted to be his Cherries Jubilee, flaming and all.

After a strong cup of coffee, I pulled on my Apex work shirt and headed out, wishing I knew how to change things. At work, I clocked in preparing for another boring day and wondered why I'd ever liked this job. What would Stone think if he knew I worked in a mail room? I wasn't in school, wasn't any where near working for my dad, and I'd never be what he thought I was.

"Camp? What the hell? You're on time?" My boss, Andrew, walked up with his tie a bit crooked and his pants a little too tight around his ass. He shoved his plain brown hair out of his eyes and smiled with his plump lips which were his best feature.

"Yeah, I guess. Don't act so surprised. It happens."

He clapped his hand on my shoulder. "If it happened more often, you might get out of this mail room." His eyebrows bounced above his big blue eyes as he laughed. "Hey, what the hell happened to your neck?"

My hand flew up to the spot I remembered Stone biting

and sucking there. "Uh...um...I don't know."

Andrew laughed heartily and smacked my shoulder. "Got you a boyfriend finally? Well, our little Camp is growing up." He shook his head as he walked away. I knew Andrew was good hearted and his joking wasn't meant to be harsh, but his words ripped a hole in my chest like sharp claws dragging through my flesh.

Everyone wanted me to grow up and if I wanted to keep Stone I would have no other choice. Did I want to keep Stone? He was certainly hot and we had electric chemistry between us. Stone had a good job and thought about his future and did responsible things, even if he wasn't exactly where he wanted to be yet. He showed his affection readily and was damned fun to hang out with. I also couldn't stop thinking about his dark curly hair and ever-changing eyes. Yeah, I wanted to keep him and hoped he wanted to keep me as well.

"Hey, Camp! Take this up to fourth, will you?" Andrew interrupted my thoughts, handing me a small package to deliver. Back to work.

The day went by in a haze of up and down, sorting packages, wondering about my life and thinking about Stone. I wanted to make sure I was still on his mind, so I sent him a quick text.

I'll never pass a parking lot again without getting a hard-on! You've ruined me! Can't wait to do it again...

Then I committed myself to telling him the truth because it wasn't so horrible that it would ruin us unless I let it continue. I convinced myself of that and went back to work.

10 Stone

I parked on the road in front of Campbell's house, noticing his car wasn't there yet. He didn't expect me, but after his cute text earlier in the day, I had to come by. After waiting on the curb for an eternity, I went and knocked on the door.

A striking guy with wispy blondish hair falling in his face but not quite hiding his stunning green eyes answered the door. Afternoon scruff, a shade darker along his chin than his hair, lined his face. He wore unbuttoned jeans and his chest and feet were bare, giving me a feast of skin for the eyes. "'Sup?" He jerked his prominent chin up.

"Uh...I'm looking for Campbell?" This guy's self-assurance had me sweating. I didn't like this hunk hanging around with Campbell. Hell, I did not need that kind of competition, with his golden skin and sleepy smile.

The guy stretched his arm up over his head, leaning into the door. Mischief flicked across his green eyes, making me think of a cat. "He's not home yet. I'm Gavin."

I held my hand out to shake. "I'm Stone."

Gavin looked at my hand, but didn't reach out to shake it. The corner of his mouth flinched up for a second like he held back a smile. "Don't know if I should let you in. I don't know when he'll be home."

"Oh, okay. That's okay. Think he'll still be at his dad's office?"

Gavin's face changed, dark eyebrows almost meeting

above his nose. "No. Camp would never go there. He would probably slit his throat before willingly going to his dad's office. He can't stand that dick. But what am I going to say about the guy? I love living here..."

"What? I thought he worked there?" What was this guy talking about? I sort of thought that Campbell admired his father to some extent, though they might not always get along, he was following the man's footsteps, working in his office and going to law school. Wasn't he? Or Maybe that was what I wanted to believe—the picture I had built in my head. Either way, this Gavin dude wasn't making any sense. Campbell said he worked at his dad's office.

Gavin laughed, and under other circumstances, it might have been a nice sound. With my world crashing down, it sounded jarring and dissonant. "Oh, hell no. Camp wouldn't work for his dad for a million fucking bucks. He works at Apex. Hey. He should be home soon. Maybe you should come in. I was just teasing before." He jerked his head, indicating the house.

I struggled with Gavin's words. It didn't seem right. I tucked my fingers into the back pockets of my jeans with my elbows jutting out and stared at him. I tried to figure out what to do or say, but standing there on his front porch, listening to his roommate shatter my image of him, I lost all reasoning, all words, like walking through a dark forest alone at night with no light to guide me.

"Oh, here he is." Gavin gestured to the road, and I turned to see Campbell parking his shiny BMW in the driveway. He got out of the car and walked over with a serious expression on his face. He had a blue and white button up shirt slung over his bare shoulder. His blue flower tattoo stood out on his glistening chest and my dick snapped to attention, as if it were a dog sitting up for his owner coming home, just from thinking about licking it again.

"Hey!" Campbell said, looking between Gavin and me. "What's going on?"

I couldn't hold back my anger. "You tell me." Between

his sexy roommate and discrepancies about his work, and my stupid cock that still wanted him, I became territorial, sliding on the edge of a furious tantrum. I wanted to throw Campbell to the ground or against a door and mark him, claim him as mine, but a larger part of me slammed on the breaks. "So, where is it you work, Campbell?"

I heard Gavin walk into the house; he surely didn't want to be a part of this conversation. I didn't watch him go, though. My eyes were on Campbell's face. His brown eyes fell and he looked like I'd punched him in the gut.

"Wanna come inside?" He stared down at his shuffling feet, the toes of his high top sneakers digging into the grass, unable to meet my eyes. Yeah, I could see his guilt in his eyes, on his face, and the way he stood there with shoulders slumped.

"No." I needed to get to the bottom of things. I went to grab his shirt.

He pulled away with a huff. "I work at Apex," he blurted out, holding up his work shirt with the logo on it.

"Fuck. This is bullshit, Campbell." He lied. My heart splintered into a million tiny pieces.

"I didn't. Shit—" He dropped his arms, letting the shirt trail on the ground, and still he wouldn't meet my eyes. "I didn't think. It's just a shitty job. Okay?"

"No. Not okay. Look at me, Campbell."

Slowly, he lifted his eyes to finally meet mine. Those chocolaty orbs held a world of sadness and I wanted to comfort him, but I was too pissed off. "Campbell, what else have you lied about?"

"Come on Stone. It's not like that." I could hear the desperation in his voice, but choked back my concern. I had to. My heart tore apart between my raging need to comfort him and blazing anger at his deception.

"What's it like then? Huh?" I yelled at him. "I can't believe this. I thought you were different. I thought we could fucking be something. Damn you, Camp."

I heard him muttering explanations, but I pushed passed

him, bumping my shoulder into his, as I headed to my car, fury winning this round of the game.

"Stop! Damn. Stone. You don't understand," he shouted after me.

I shook my head and opened my car door, looking over the vehicle at him. "No. I don't. I don't understand at all. You-You, damn. You let me go on and on about your job and your future. And you lied. Lied. To my face. You broke my fucking heart." My voice choked in my throat. "Why?"

"I don't know. I've never been in love before and it's kind of got me doing stupid things. I don't understand it either. Shit. I'm really fucking up here and I don't know what to do."

Unfair. That was so unfair. I glared at Campbell. He was the first guy I ever let jerk me around like this. I wanted him and his words about love, but at the same time they were like choking on something bitter. I got in my car and drove away, unable to deal with him.

Love?

What the hell did he know about love?

11 Campbell

"What the hell happened?" Julien asked, when I drug my sorry ass into the living room and dropped to the couch in a huff. "Camp?"

"It's over. He busted me before I could fess up." I hated how whiny I sounded.

"Fuck," Julien muttered.

"Yeah, Fuck. I'm totally fucked."

He stood in front of me for a minute, just looking at me and making me feel like melting under his accusing glare.

"Okay. Go get cleaned up. I'm taking you out for dinner. You need comfort food."

I dragged myself up and into my room without arguing. I didn't have it in me. After I cleaned up and headed for the front door, I noticed Gavin's door was still shut. He probably regretted opening his mouth and didn't want to face me, but it was my own fault. I shouldn't have lied in the first place and ultimately, I missed many opportunities to straighten out the story. Yet I didn't feel generous enough to let him off the hook yet, so I slammed the door hard as I left. *Real mature, Camp.*

Julien shot daggers at me as we walked out to his car. We drove through town in silence, but my head churned with all the ways this relationship with Stone had gone wrong.

When Julien turned north on South Florida instead of continuing on to Channelside, I figured we were going to Malio's, his favorite steak house. He circled around Twiggs and down Ashley and parked at the little restaurant behind the Sykes building, which the locals called the Beer Can for its tall cylindrical presence in the center of town. The river rolled by lazily in perfect view from the parking lot. I bet it looked even better from the top of the Sykes building, but we weren't going there.

Since we didn't have reservations, we were able to get seated at one of the high top tables lined up beside the bar. White table cloths covered the tables and were topped with candles in a glass holder that flickered, giving the room a nice warm, yet modern feel around the amber floors and caramel colored booths. They could have been serving on paper plates and the place would still be packed. Julien had brought me here several times, so I knew the food would be divine regardless of what I ordered.

We started with fancy martinis and oysters on the half shell, but I knew Julien would insist on steak for the main course. That's what you went to Malio's for after all.

When the server took the oyster mess away, Julien finally spoke up. "So, what happened?"

I shrugged. "Guess Gavin accidentally spilled the beans." I sipped my drink waiting for Julien to say something else. After a moment, I had to open my own fat mouth. "So? You gonna say you told me so?"

"No. I don't need to. You know where you screwed up. I don't have to tell you. But, seriously, you can't keep doing this—"

"I know," I growled, interrupting him. "I do know. Time to grow up, huh? I'm trying. I just don't know what I'm doing and I don't know how to be a fucking grown up."

Julien sighed deeply and slid his empty glass across the table. He motioned for the waiter to bring him another. "Hey, who's that?"

"Who?"

"Guy over there keeps staring at you." He nodded to a booth farther down from us and I turned to look as the waiter sat two more drinks in front of us.

"You ready to order, guys?"

I stared at the guy who tried to pretend he hadn't been looking at us, while Julien ordered a couple of New York Strips. When the waiter walked away, I turned back to Julien.

"He looks a lot like the guy that lost his shit at my dad's office the other day."

"Oh?" Julien lifted his martini glass, sipping politely.

I took a larger swallow. "Huh? Yeah. Dad said he didn't get the settlement he expected and was pissed, but he's eating here." I knew damn well our steaks were going to be fifty bucks each. Any meal at Malio's would be expensive as hell. We didn't eat here often, mostly because Julien insisted on paying, which raised my guilt levels a few notches. Not tonight, though.

"Forget that dude, Camp. What are you going to do about Stone?"

I stared over at my best friend, wishing I had better answers and wishing I could be more like him. "I don't know. I guess I'll call him and try to sort it out."

"I hope you can, but if not? Take this as a lesson learned because Stone seemed like a great guy, someone worth keeping around."

His words kicked me in my already sore gut. "You don't have to tell me that." My style had never been moping, but losing Stone and knowing it had been my own damn fault, had everything in my world fucked up. Being honest with myself, Stone had rocked my world from the first second I laid eyes on him, and I hadn't been myself from that moment. I'd lost all my "cool" on first sight.

Julien set his glass down and leaned forward. "That guy's still looking at you."

I snickered a little. "You'd think he would have something better to do. I'm not that interesting."

"Oh, hell no. You're interesting. Like watching a freak show," Julien teased.

"Fuck you, meanie."

"Meanie? Huh? That's all you've got? Meanie? Yep.

You're totally fucked, Camp."

I couldn't help but laugh at him and with the tension broken, Julien spent the rest of the evening keeping the conversation away from anything that would make me think about Stone. I appreciated the gesture, but when he took a quick trip to the restroom, I called Stone. He didn't answer and I left a mellow voicemail, simply asking if we could talk.

After the steak, Julien ordered a cheesecake slice to split. By the time we left, Julien's wallet was almost two hundred bucks lighter and I was stuffed with the best food in town. Back at his car, I stretched the seatbelt across my waist and chest and clicked it in place. "Jay. Thanks."

"Not a problem, dude. You know you're like my brother. I'd do just about anything for you."

With a sigh, I leaned my forehead against the cool glass, refusing to look at the lack of messages on my phone. Half way home, I gave in and peeked. Nothing. I dialed him again, but when his voicemail picked up, I ended the call without leaving a message.

Julien glanced over at me quickly before shifting his gaze back to the road. "He's not answering?"

"No."

"Sorry, dude. Give him a little space and time. He may come around."

"No, I don't think he will," I huffed. I'd blown it with Stone for sure. Great, just one more thing to fucking hate myself for.

12 Stone

Saturday rolled around like a rock for a crack addict and I knew if I was going to stop myself from answering Campbell's calls, I had to get the hell out of town. I needed distraction. I just wasn't ready to deal with any of it.

After a quick shower, I searched for my comfort clothes and pulled on cotton sweats over my athletic shorts and a loose tank top. I grabbed my hoodie and headed out the door. Half an hour later, I walked into my folk's house in Plant City.

Harley, the youngest of my siblings jumped up off the couch. "Dude!" he hollered and jumped me, practically climbing up my shoulders until I dumped him on the couch.

"Hey, man, stop. Where's everybody?"

Harley shrugged, leaning back into the couch. "We haven't seen you in like forever, man. I think Dad's at work and Mom's, you know, Mom. Running around."

"Blaze?"

Harley rolled his eyes up, nudging his head toward the second floor. "Still sleeping, probably. He came home late. Senior party or some shit." He sounded just a tad jealous.

"Yeah? Well, don't sweat it. You'll be there next year, baby boy. Let's go throw the ball around or something."

"You did not come here just to play ball with me. What's up?"

"Nothing."

Harley flipped himself around and jumped me again. This

time he had me in a headlock in about three seconds, but I stood up and dumped his ass on the couch again and followed up by pinning his arms behind his head and digging my elbow into his ribs.

He laughed and screeched and shoved me around, attempting to fight back, but I had a good thirty pounds of muscle on his scrawny ass. "You need to hit the weights, little bro."

He squealed again, as I got him under the arm.

"Shut the fuck up!" Came Blaze's grumpy yelling from upstairs.

"Make me, you little shit!" I hollered back.

In a minute, Blaze came flying down the stairs and they were ganging up on me. I'd missed my brothers more than I had thought. When they both had me pinned and sufficiently tickled, I groaned and gave up. "Uncle! Stop, stop!"

"That's what you get for never coming around here, asshole," Blaze griped.

"Hey, everything okay?"

Blaze nodded and smiled. "Yeah, it's great. I'm taking Felicia Hernandez to prom."

I punched him in the shoulder, not knowing who she was, but happy for him anyway. "So? This is a good thing, right?"

"Hell, yeah! She's so hot, man!"

Harley rolled his eyes.

"What about you? You going to prom?" I butted my shoulder into his, while Blaze grabbed a football and we made our way to the back yard.

"No, I'm not going to stupid prom."

"Hey, Harley...wait. Why not? You're a good looking kid with great genes, if I do say so myself." I wiggled my eyebrows at him. "Go long, Blaze!"

The older of the two ran the length of the yard and I popped a perfect spiral right to him. "I still got it." I smacked Harley on the shoulder. "So?"

He kicked at the grass, looking dejected. "My boyfriend doesn't want to go. It's you know...this place kind of sucks.

The kids are dicks, mostly."

Blaze threw the football back and I caught it, but then dropped it, staring at Harley. "What? Boyfriend?"

"Yes, boyfriend. I'm gay." He wouldn't look at me.

Had I let him down by not sticking around and being a better role model for him? Going to high school at Armwood had been just as bad, if not worse for a gay kid. It might have been closer to the city than his school, but it still had its share of rednecks and people that didn't want to tolerate differences. I dealt with it, then got the hell out of there. Maybe I didn't share enough with him; maybe I needed to share more. "Harley. I'm gay. I get it."

"You say that, but I've never met any of your boyfriends."

Blaze marched back across the yard, scowling at us. "Geez with the gay drama. Fuck the rest of the world. I told you I'd have your back, dude. Take Brock to the fucking prom already."

"He won't go. He won't even go on a real fucking date with me. Stone? What do I do?"

"I don't know. Maybe you need to try and understand how he feels. It's scary being openly gay around here sometimes."

"Even for you?"

"Sure, yeah. But at least you have Blaze watching out for you."

Harley dropped to the ground, crossing his legs and planting his elbows on his knees. "I really like Brock."

"Geez!" Blaze groaned and rolled his eyes. "I'm getting some sodas. Want one?"

"Yes, please." I sat down on the ground beside Harley. "He's not giving you a hard time is he?" I jerked my thumb toward the direction Blaze had just gone.

"Nah, not like that. He just hates drama. He's been really cool. He even offered to double date with us."

"Hmm. That's nice."

He bumped his shoulder into mine. "I'd rather double with you, though. Don't you have a boyfriend? For real, you got the Medlock genes too."

"I don't know. I thought I did, but..."

Blaze walked out and handed us a can of soda each. "But what Stone?"

"Guess, we broke up."

"Ahh...I don't really want to hear about your relationships, but uh, yeah, that sucks, dude." Blaze joined us on the ground. "Not to change the subject and all, but Mom's gonna be home soon. She's gonna freak when she sees you."

"It hasn't been that long since I've been here."

Harley jumped up. "Hey we should call Sissy! It'll be a real family reunion."

"It hasn't been that long." They always teased me and our sister, Brooke, when we showed up at home. Only Harley called her Sissy. "Brooke is not going to drive out here at the last minute anyway. So, chill."

That's when Mom came out in the back yard and squealed like a teenager. "Stone! Oh my God! Where have you been? We all thought you were dead! *OhmyGod*!"

My brothers laughed at her antics as she grabbed me in a huge hug, strangling me with her arms around my throat. "God, Mom. Come on!" I peeled her off of me and she laughed with my brothers.

"Don't be so serious, Son. Come on inside and let's catch up. I brought a couple pizzas for lunch."

We spent time together, eating and chatting about what everyone had been up to. My brothers told me about their grades and friends and extracurricular activities. And Brock and Felicia. Both my brothers were smitten with their new romantic interests. I couldn't stop thinking about Campbell. He would so get along with my goofy family. I could easily imagine him here with us. "You seem quiet, Stone." My mom slid another piece of pizza in front of me.

I shrugged and took a big bite so I wouldn't have to answer her, but Harley jumped right in. "He's sad 'cause he just broke up with his boyfriend."

"Oh? I didn't know you had a boyfriend. Was it serious?"

I let out a long deep, overly dramatic sigh. "I thought so, but he lied to me."

"About what?"

Harley leaned in to listen, but Blaze kept stuffing his face.

"Where he works, what he does for a living. That's like lying about who he is." I took a swallow of Coke, hoping to hide how choked up I'd started getting over talking about it.

"Maybe. Maybe not." My mom leaned back in her chair and glared at me. "So, where did you meet him? Uh, what's his name?"

"Campbell. And I met him in a bar." I rolled my eyes just knowing what they were going to say about that. "It's almost the only way to meet other gay guys, Mom."

"I didn't say anything."

"No, but you were thinking it."

"Now, Stone Rhett Medlock! How do you know what the hell I was thinking?"

Shit! She used all three names. My mouth opened, eyes widened. I realized I'd lied to Campbell, too. I didn't tell him my middle name, claiming not to have one, but really? Rhett? Please. My name was a joke and I wanted him to take me seriously. "I don't know."

Mom gave me a knowing look. "Don't know what, Stone?"

"Maybe we just didn't get off to a good start. He's...He's Campbell Fain as in Fain, Montgomery, Forsyth. Maybe that was a lot of pressure for just meeting someone."

"Stone..."

"I'm not saying it's okay, Mom. Lying is not okay. Just...what you say to someone you're just starting a relationship with and what you might say to someone that's just a hookup—"

"Stone!" My mom reached over and put her hands over Harley's ears.

All of us boys just groaned. "Please, Mom," Harley fussed. "I know about hookups, already."

She swatted his arm. "You better not be doing hookups!"

"No way, I'm in love with Brock already!"

Mom nudged him with her elbow and wiggled her eyebrows to let him know she was kidding. My mom had always been fun like that, kidding and joking around. I loved her for her quirkiness.

Blaze interrupted. "So, what about these hookups?"

I rolled my eyes and pushed my plate away. My family could really be exhausting. "Listen, I just meant it isn't always easy to know who's going to be just for the moment and who might last longer. So, maybe he didn't know..."

"Seriously, Stone," she said, reaching across the table. "Does he mean something to you? Maybe you should try and work things out. Give him a second chance?"

"I don't know. It hurts that he lied. But, it's worse that he didn't tell me about it later. You know? I would have understood, but he waited until he got caught out."

"Dude, that sucks," Harley said. "I'd be pissed."

"Pissed and hurt." And still with no answers. I missed him and I wanted him, but I couldn't trust him and that didn't make a relationship.

Mom tapped her fingers on the table. "Uh...Stone. I have to say this. Maybe you didn't give him enough credit. Maybe, you weren't realistic?"

I dropped my pizza slice on the paper plate in front of me. "What? What do you mean?"

"Face it, Stone. Sometimes you don't live in the same world as the rest of us. It's like you build things up to unrealistic proportions. Maybe he couldn't live up to that."

"She's right." Blaze snagged the half-eaten slice from my plate.

"She's not right. That's crazy."

My mom looked at me with raised eyebrows. I knew that look. It meant she thought I was full of shit.

I held my hands up, resigned. I didn't know what she meant, but if there was some truth in it, I needed to consider it. "Okay. Whatever."

She shook her head, as if unsure I really took her serious,

as she started cleaning up the table.

I hung out with my brothers a while longer and we tossed the football around the rest of the afternoon before heading upstairs for some Xbox. Eventually, dad came home and we ate dinner and goofed around. All too soon, though, time to leave crept around. I didn't know how the next day or even one more night would go without him, but at least I'd had a day to relax with my family.

Walking out to my car, Harley called out to me. I turned and waited for him to catch up. "'Sup, dude?"

"Uh...thanks for the advice earlier."

I chuckled and tossed my arm around his shoulder. "I didn't say anything much."

"No, but you know?"

"No. What?" I leaned against the car and watched Harley shift his weight from foot to foot. "What? Really?"

"Just, thanks for being you and don't stay away so long. Maybe bring this boyfriend home to meet us. Let us know when and I'll invite Brock over. Maybe? Please?"

"You want to show him that other gay guys exist in Central Florida?"

"Maybe. Something like that." He stuffed his hands in the front pockets of his jeans.

"Okay. I get it." I took a deep breath and thought about Campbell. "You'd like him, you know."

"Yeah! So? You going to get back with him?"

"We'll see." I gave my brother a big hug and then drove home. I turned the radio off and just thought about things, about Campbell, and that maybe I should give him another chance. I missed his face and his bleached blond hair. He always had a quick smile and I loved the way he laughed. But who was he really? He wasn't a law student working at his father's firm. So, who was Campbell Fain?

13 Campbell

Monday morning sucked.

I'd spent the entire weekend drunk, trying not to think about Stone, but the more I'd tried not to think about him, the more I'd thought about him. Thinking about not thinking about him had driven me to the bars, but I didn't find him there. I'd found plenty of alcohol, though. I woke with a pounding headache worthy of three days of nonstop drinking for sure. I thought about calling in sick, but where would that get me except another long day of thinking about not thinking about Stone and drinking more because I couldn't stop thinking about him. *Fuck my life.*

After a long hot shower and four Tylenol, I dressed and crawled behind the wheel of my BMW, wondering if going in to work was a mistake and how would I know before I actually made it in. Seemed like I lived my life that way, after all, jumping first and worrying about mistakes later. I scoffed at myself and headed for work.

When I turned on Kennedy to head into the downtown area, I noticed a big gray van pulling on the road behind me. It looked vaguely familiar; must belong to one of my neighbors. When I turned North on Florida Avenue, the van followed. A weird feeling crept over me and the hair on the back of my neck prickled.

After a moment I chastised myself. Paranoia as a result of too much weekend binging should be ignored, so I shook it off. But when I pulled into the private parking at the Apex building, I looked in my rearview mirror and saw the van pass by on Polk and wondered if he had been following me after all. Yet, a lot of folks in my neighborhood and surrounding areas worked in Tampa. I parked, paying attention and making sure the van didn't enter the garage.

I swallowed hard and put my hand over my chest where I could feel my heart hammering. Silly how I worked myself up over nothing, so I laughed, but it sounded a bit uncanny.

I got out of the car and practically raced to the elevator, telling myself that I'd just overloaded my nerves. *Crappy ass hangover.* Once at work, I didn't think about it anymore.

The glaring fluorescents stabbed my eyes while I sorted mail, making me hate my job when I never really had before. I bitched and moaned through most of the day until Andrew called me into the break room for a chat.

"What's going on with you, Camp?" He pulled out a chair and the scrape across the linoleum ground through my brain.

"Had a rough weekend, boss."

He took a tentative sip of coffee, watching me over the rim. "Really? Seems like more than that." His mouth took up half his face when he smiled wide like that.

"What do you mean?" I so did not want to have this conversation, especially since my head weighed a ton, my mouth dried up like the Sahara, and my gut wanted to do summersaults if I moved too fast. I pulled another pack of Tylenol out of my pocket and swallowed the pills with lukewarm coffee and blanched.

Andrew leaned back in his chair. "You're normally a lot bubblier. You've been kind of moping for the past week or so. What gives? Not happy here anymore? Finally getting some ambition?"

"Honestly, I'm trying to grow up a little, but it's really not easy. Seriously? It sucks."

"So, why do it?"

No, I really didn't want to talk about this with him. "Maybe it is time to move up. What would I need to do to get out of the mailroom?"

Andrew smiled again, cracking his face open. He was the type of boss that liked promoting people, as long as they promoted out of his department and didn't take his job. "Well, Campbell. There are entry level openings all over the place. Data entry, admin." He shrugged and sipped his coffee again. "You could also go back to school."

"Hm..." I got up to refill my mug. Thank the gods of bosses for free coffee.

"Even openings in legal. If that's what you want." I heard his mug slide across the table and sensed his eyes staring into the back of my head as I poured the coffee. "Is that what you want?"

I turned around to face him. "Hell if I know."

"Maybe you should figure that out first. Lots of opportunity at Apex for a smart kid like you." He pointed at me and his eyebrows rose as he spoke. "In fact, Camp, I'm sure you'll do well anywhere. But..."

"What?"

"You need to decide what you want before moving forward. You know? Otherwise, you'd just be wasting your time. No sense in making a move, especially an expensive one like school, without having a solid goal. Do you even want to work here?"

"What do you mean? Why wouldn't I want to work here?"

"Sit down, Camp." He kicked out a chair, unaware of how the noise clawed at my brain, making me cringe.

I sat down quickly, before he could do it again.

"Campbell. Don't you want to go into law? I mean, you could go into law and still work here. Apex hires all kinds of lawyers. Employment law pays well."

"I don't want to follow in my dad's footsteps."

Andrew waved his hand in the air. "Your dad does malpractice. You could do something else, still be in law and not be following his footsteps. Employment law is different. Criminal law is different. I'm just saying."

"You sound like Julien."

"Well, he must be a smart chap." Andrew winked at me and broke out that mammoth smile one-more-fucking-time.

I rubbed my face with my hands. "My dad's firm does employment law and about a dozen other things." They were known primarily for the malpractice because that's where they made most of their money—winning big cases.

"Well, I'm just saying that you need to think about this. If you aren't happy here or if growing up means moving on...just...get a plan first. Okay?"

I nodded and sipped my coffee, concentrating on the heat of the cup against my palm rather than the rest of my life.

"Okay. Pep talk over. Get back to work, buddy. And try smiling a little. Might help you get through the day." He patted my shoulder on his way out the door. *Happy fucker!*

"Back to work. Right."

I made my rounds throughout the building with Andrew's words on my mind. With Stone on my mind. He still hadn't returned any of my calls and texts and I knew I had two choices. Either give up or find some other way to get to him. I knew he had a romantic side. Sending me those lilies proved it. I had to send him something that made him remember me, see me, not just my name on his phone.

With that settled, I called my dad's office. Andrew was right about having a plan. I just didn't know how to go about getting one. Karen, the receptionist, answered the phone. "Hey, K-baby!" I teased her.

"Campbell Fain. Stop harassing me, you little shit. What do you want, boy?"

I could always count on Karen to tease me back. "I need an appointment with my dad."

"Oh. My. God! Did the earth just move? Is the temperature rising? Surely hell has come!"

"What?"

"Maybe I didn't hear you right, because the Campbell Fain I know? Seriously, he doesn't *willingly* visit his father."

I gave her a fake laugh. Even though she was playing

around, she was also right. For once, this was different. Since I'd met Stone, everything was different. "Yeah, yeah...play all you want, but I'm serious. I need time on his calendar."

"Okay, sugar. Let me pull up his schedule, but warn a girl next time. Shesh! I'm getting too old for a heart attack." After a bit more banter, we made an appointment for Wednesday after work. I needed to talk seriously with my dad about my life. He needed to help me find a career.

On my way home, I noticed the same gray van parked along the side of the street. It looked like someone had written in the dirt along the side panel and then wiped it away. A small crack in the center of the windshield had just started to spider out. For a second, I thought I should get the license plate number. Then I shook my head and made my way across town. I needed to get home and figure out what I could send Stone to get his attention.

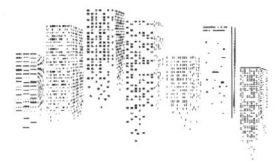

I fired up my laptop and quickly found the perfect gift. It didn't say I'm sorry or I love you in a blatant way, but it did say that I paid attention and I knew him at least a little. The retro-gamer pack cost me a pretty penny, but I would have paid twice that for Stone. The gift box came with two classic Nintendo games and a shit-ton of snacks. Perfect.

With my gift ordered, I made my way into the bathroom. My headache had finally eased up and I thought I would just get cleaned up and ready for the next day, maybe even go to bed early. I splashed water on my face and peered into the mirror. For once, I saw what my father saw. A punk. A kid. How could anyone ever take me seriously? My dark eyes seemed sad. I took out my gauge and the loops that lined the rim of my left ear. I couldn't do anything about the hair, except wait and let it grow out. Once it got a little longer, I could cut it and most of the blond would be gone, replaced by mouse brown. The thought depressed me a little. I didn't want to be mouse anything...I was Campbell Fain, rebel, fun guy, ever-flirty, the trickster.

I frowned into the mirror. I didn't like that Campbell Fain anymore. That Campbell Fain was also full of himself, deceitful and lonely. Stone would never fall for that guy. I bit my bottom lip, hating how pouty it looked and regretting the gift I'd sent. Maybe it sent the wrong message after all.

14 Stone

I played Campbell's voicemail message. Again. He sounded sincere, but then he always sounded sincere, but what the hell did I really know about it? He lied to my face with that same sincere voice with his beseeching eyes looking into my soul. How could I believe him? Now or ever?

Rubbing my chest, I leaned back and listened one more time.

"Stone. Please. Let's just talk about this. I thought we had something worth saving. Something special. Call me."

He hadn't even said sorry. He didn't apologize in his voicemail or the thirty something texts he sent. So, how could I consider calling him back?

Maybe I missed his spark of playfulness in my life. I tended to be too serious, melodramatic. I could feel the skin around my mouth pull tighter with my frown. In the short time we'd been together, Campbell had lit up my dark world. For once, I had something besides work and Xbox.

Why had I expected more from him, anyway? I had told myself I wouldn't be picking up any club-rats and that's just what I did. That made it my own damn fault. I should never have...but it had been fun and Campbell's laugh sounded like that Christmas story about angel's getting their wings when the bell rang, except my own heart had gained the feathers and thought it could fly.

I needed to figure out what I'd give to have that sound

back in my life every day. Could I just get over it? Could I put my heart back on the chopping block? I'd forgiven him already, even without him asking; that wasn't the problem. Making myself vulnerable when I knew he could do it again; that was the problem.

Then there was what my mom said about it. Did I set the bar so high that Campbell could never really reach it? Even though that might be possible, it still didn't excuse the lying. Being truthful was not something unattainable in a relationship. Besides all that, I'd liked him before he told me he was going to be a lawyer like his old man. Didn't I?

I sighed and dragged my moping ass off the couch. Ultimately, I wanted Campbell back. I missed those big brown eyes and the smile that lit up not only his face but the whole fucking room and my own miserable soul.

I tapped Campbell's picture in my contact list. The ring tone sounded. The call rolled to his voicemail.

I did it again.

I wouldn't be ignored. Once I had my mind fixed on something, I usually persisted until I got what I wanted, so I washed my face in the bathroom and pulled on slightly nicer clothes, black jeans and a short sleeved button down, and shoved my feet in my Nikes. Twenty minutes later, I parked my Honda at the curb in front of his house. His pretty Beemer sat in the driveway, so I knew he was home. Swallowing hard, I got out and marched across the front lawn.

The door opened to a plain guy, around my height with short dark hair and brown eyes that shined like candy, much darker than Campbell's. I kind of recognized him as the other roommate, but couldn't remember his name.

"Hey, I know you!" he gasped and pointed at me.

"You do? I'm here for Campbell."

"Oh man! You played QB for Armwood. Few years back. Y'all went to State that year. Yeah." He snapped his fingers. "You had one of the best touchdown to interception rates in history. My cousins said if you threw the ball, nothing but red zone, dude!"

"Your cousins?"

"Yeah, they went to Brandon. Frankie was a decent tight end that year for them. Nice to meet you. I'm Tony." He spat his words out like a machine gun.

I shook his hand. "Stone Medlock. I'm surprised anybody remembers my stats."

"Oh, I do. I have a thing for stats, especially when they're outside of the norm."

"'Kay. Thanks. I'm still looking for Campbell…"

"Oh, right. He ain't here."

I looked over my shoulder at his car.

"That means he's probably drinking."

That thought didn't settle well in my stomach. The thought of Campbell going to a bar without me had me growling low in my throat.

"I have no idea when he'll be back. Jay-Jay might know, but he's still at work, which means Camp probably went out on his own. At least he's smart enough not to drink and drive. DUI arrests have been up about four percent this year over the past couple years. But Orange County is the worst. They had over 3,000 arrests last year." His eyebrows rose as he spoke his steady stream of information that no one asked for.

"Okay. Thanks." I turned my back to him and stared at Campbell's car. I knew he had some common sense and his dad was a pretty famous lawyer, so surely some of that rubbed off on him—or not. I snorted, and headed back to my car. Now I was on a mission.

I followed the trail of bars that led from Campbell's house to mine, skipping only the most unlikely places for Campbell to go. After five failed attempts, I gave in and drove to the Dragon Club, where we'd met and where my gut told me I'd find him.

Even on a week night, the colored lights were bouncing around the pulsing dance floor. The bass pounded through my head, reverberating through my body, making me want to puke as it jumped in my stomach. Mostly men dominated the floor, but there were a few girls too, all of them grinding on each other and waving their arms around, bouncing at the knees in time with that overpowering bass beat. I saw a few blonds, but none were Campbell.

I made my way around to the bar, looking around, searching the faces reflected with pink, purple, and red from the disco lights. Across the bar, I met his eyes. He froze, his face set in a scowl, but his eyes were questioning.

I sighed heavily, and made my way around the bar. He never took his eyes off me. Despite everything, I was important to him. That much was unmistakable.

"Stone, you're here!" he leaned in and yelled in my ear.

I grabbed his arm firmly, but not tight enough to hurt. "Let's go talk outside." I nodded to the entrance and Campbell smiled his agreement.

An empty shot glass sat on the bar in front of him, and he smelled like alcohol. As we walked to the front of the bar, he was a little unsteady, wobbly even. I supported him with a grip on his shoulder a few times before we made it outside.

"Stone," he sighed and leaned against my side, his body fitting to mine, as soon as we were out the door.

I wrapped my arm around him. "Campbell, we need to talk about this, but I'm thinking this isn't the best time."

"Please. Let's talk. I miss you." His body wiggled against me, giving me an instant hard-on.

I had to shove at his shoulders. "Stop."

"'Kay." Campbell pulled away from me, leaned to the side, straightened and leaned again.

"You alright?"

"Fine. So?"

Before I could stop myself, I blurted out, "Why'd you lie to me?"

Campbell sucked his bottom lip between his teeth and righted himself, though I could tell it took effort. He was obviously pretty drunk. "Damn, Stone. I wanted to tell you the truth. I just couldn't take you looking at me like that."

"Like what?"

"Like that, like you are now, like I'm nothing." His words

ran together, slurring from the alcohol.

"Campbell, don't." I didn't like him putting himself down, especially when he thought that's how I felt. I didn't.

"No. You don't. I'm a screw up. I know it. My dad knows it. Everyone knows it. I'm nothing. I just didn't want you to think that. Just for a little while. Can't you understand that?"

I shook my head and stared at the ground. "That's bullshit, Campbell. Self-loathing is not you."

"You don't know me!" he yelled. "I have a fucking associate's degree and a crap job in a mail room. I'm nothing. I'm not studying law. I hate law. I hate my fucking dad. You don't know. You don't—"

"Stop yelling. Damn it!" He'd never given me the chance to know him. I'd only known what I thought he was, what I wanted him to be. I had no idea who Campbell really was.

He ignored me. "You're fucking perfect and you'll never get it. You don't know anything about me! I just wanted you to see me." He finally stopped yelling, but turned to walk away.

"Where are you going? I'm trying to work this out, Campbell." I gave him a second chance, and he just walked away. I couldn't fathom it. This was simply not how it was supposed to go.

Campbell didn't answer, he just flung his hand up at me and kept walking. He had to deal with his own issues and we were getting nowhere arguing while he was drunk outside of the Dragon Club. I let him walk away, but it was one of the hardest things I'd ever done. Every instinctive urge inside me wanted to follow him and make sure he got home safe. Yet, he was a big boy and had to learn to take care of himself. He needed to figure it out.

I got in my car and went home to a night of staring at the ceiling and wondering how this relationship had gotten so off track. Was my mom right? Did I make all of this out to be something it wasn't? Campbell had lied, but I was left feeling like I needed to apologize.

15 Campbell

What the hell had I done? As soon as the alarm clock blared out, I knew I'd royally screwed my life up. Stone had given me a chance to explain and I fucking blew it. I pounded the clock until it stopped and dropped my arm over my face. I had to be the king-loser of the world.

Getting up and on with it was inevitable, but I would rather have pulled my pillow over my head and vegged out under the covers than face my pathetic life, especially since my head would not stop pounding. Fucking hangover on top of everything. I hoped I'd be feeling better before I had to face my dad...at my own request. Could I back out of that?

Reluctantly, I made my way to the shower. With hot water pouring over my rebellious body, I thought about my big screw up. Stone had been there, right in front of me, and what did I do? Yell at him as if it had all been his fault. I'd been sitting at the bar slamming back shots and feeling utterly sorry for myself when he showed up and I let him feel my anger, but it should have been directed inward. I wondered what he thought about that.

I'd caught a cab a few blocks away from the bar and realized my phone had been off and I'd missed two calls from him before he found me at Dragon Club. Maybe if I'd had that warning...I couldn't deal with what-if's. I needed to pack the drama club away and just deal. *Get on with it princess!*

After getting ready for work, I made it to the kitchen to

pour me a cup of coffee. Julien sat at the bar, eating breakfast. "Morning, Camp." I glared at his overly cheerful face over my cup. "What the hell's wrong with you?"

I didn't answer him. What the hell was I supposed to say? Yes, Julien, I fucked up. Again.

Gavin walked out of his room, humming pleasantly under his breath, making me feel like throwing my cup at him. "Hey, y'all! Oh, Tony said that football-guy came by here looking for you last night."

"Football guy?" I needed to know who he was talking about—needed to know if it was *him*.

"Yeah...uh, Stone...that guy." Gavin snapped his fingers at me.

Julien perked up. "Football?"

"He played in high school or something," Gavin answered.

I didn't care about football or when he played. "When was he here?"

"Uh, guess about an hour or so after you left."

"Fuck." I sipped my coffee, wanting to hide behind the mug.

Julien's eyes narrowed. "Did you find him last night?"

I sighed and peered at him over the mug. "Yes."

"And?"

"What do you think? I fucked it up. I blew it. Happy?"

Julien grumbled, "What the hell, Camp?"

He wasn't my fucking father and this didn't concern him. "Fuck off, Jay-Jay. Really." I dropped my mug to the counter.

Julien threw a piece of toast at me. "Hey, Camp. I'm on your side, dude. I want you to be happy. Okay? And you're like fucking yourself—sideways. Pull your head out of your ass already."

"You don't know a god-damned thing about it."

"I know you."

I lifted one eyebrow at him and he threw another piece of toast.

"Come on, Camp. Don't you think it's time to grow up?"

"What...? I don't see *you* with a boyfriend. And who's the one throwing food?"

"No boyfriend yet, but I'm going to be damned ready when I meet him...and I'm sure as hell not going to lie to him."

That was the last thing I needed to hear. Him holding up a mirror so I could see the ugly beast I'd become? Well, fuck him. I could hold that mirror up all by myself. I shoved my coffee mug across the counter and stormed off before I said something I knew I'd regret.

I heard Julien calling after me, but I couldn't stop—not an option. I drove to work mad at him, mad at me, and mad at the whole fucking world. I didn't even stop for a Tylenol when there was undeniably somebody pounding out the Calypso on a giant set of bongos inside my head.

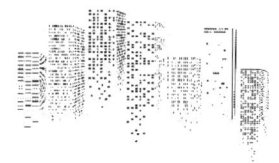

With the work day over, I made my way through crappy traffic, heading over to my father's office over on Westshore. I ended up being a good fifteen minutes late thanks to an accident on I-275, but I should have expected that. There's always an accident on the highway.

My dad's office comforted me for once, like going home. Kimmy leaned over the front desk, working on something with the receptionist, Karen. "Working late again, ladies?" I asked, getting their attention. They both smiled brightly at me.

"Hey, Camp. Your dad's waiting for you. Go on back," Karen said nodding to the hallway leading to my dad's office.

"Thanks, Special K!"

"Hey!" Kimmy wasn't going to let me get away with flirting with Karen without flirting with her too. "What do I look like here?"

"Ah! You know I love you both! You're both like my favorite Kit-Kat!"

Kim rolled her eyes and Karen giggled.

"More like Kim-Kat!" I added with a wink, but I didn't feel like playing with them. I needed to get this conversation with my dad over with.

I tapped on the door, then opened it. "Dad?"

"Yeah. Come on in Camp. Sit." He motioned to the chairs in front of his desk, then to my surprise, he walked around his desk and sat in one of them, and pushed the other around for me to sit down. "What's this about?"

I sat next to him. Claustrophobia had my skin crawling with the proximity; he sat entirely too close. "I...I...uh, Dad? Guess I need some advice."

"You never come to me for advice." He screwed his face up, looking very perplexed.

I couldn't look him in the eye. I didn't want him to be right. "I know. But, see...this is different."

"Different how?"

I took a deep breath and let it out before answering. I let my shoulders slump, defeated. "You know I met someone. We talked about—"

"A female someone or a male someone?"

"Are you in denial or what? My God, Dad! I already told you I have a boyfriend. Why does it matter anyway? Does it have to matter?"

My dad leaned back in his chair and put his hands behind his neck with elbows pointing out. "That means it's the male someone. I was hoping you'd met...someone else..."

I rubbed nervously at my forehead. The conversation had rambled off in the wrong direction. "Look, Dad. I just want to know how I figure out about finding a career. I don't want to be a lawyer like you, okay? But I want to be more than a mail clerk. So, how do I figure it out?"

"Campbell, son. You have to explore. Try something new. Take some classes. This isn't hard."

"Yes, it is. Andrew said I should figure it out before I make any moves, so I don't waste time on shit I don't want to do."

"Andrew?"

"My boss."

My dad gave me a curt nod. "This isn't the new boyfriend, then?"

"There's no boyfriend."

"You said you met someone."

We'd jump off track again. "Yeah, but he's not really my boyfriend. Listen, thanks. Very helpful advice." I didn't mean to sound sarcastic, but the need to defend my situation with Stone had the words coming out all wrong. I stood up to leave.

"Camp, wait. Look. Maybe you should take some time to write down things you like. Maybe you'll find a pattern there and an area to pursue further. Sometimes, we need to put it on paper. Black and white." He moved his hands back and forth as he spoke.

I perked up at that suggestion. "Okay. I like that idea. Thanks."

"Did you really come all the way out here for just that?"

I shrugged. "It didn't sound like a phone call conversation."

"I'm glad you're finally thinking about your future, Camp. I'm behind you on that. Maybe if you make a decent career move, you'll see Lorain as more than a friend."

"Uh, no. Never. This is about Stone."

"Stone?"

I plopped back down in the chair. How did I get my dad to realize I was gay and that was never going to change? "Dad. Stone Medlock is the guy I met. I told you about him already. But he's a serious sort. He's...you know? He's special and I don't want to lose him, but I think I already have."

"Because you don't have a decent career? He can't be that great if he left you because you work in the mail room, Camp. There is nothing wrong with working in the mail room."

"He didn't. I mean, it wasn't like that. It was me."

He shook his head. "I don't understand you at all."

"I took the mailroom job to get back at you. I didn't want to be a lawyer or anything else you wanted. I liked the job though." I shrugged. "But when I met Stone. It didn't feel like it was enough. Like it'd been this stupid prank and it wasn't...I wasn't good enough for him." I looked down at my Chucks. Maybe I needed a more grown up pair of shoes too.

"Camp...never think that. You're good enough for anybody. But if you can't be proud of your choices, you need to re-evaluate what you're doing."

"I know. I am. That's why I'm here."

My dad peered at me with lowered brows and pursed his lips together. He leaned forward resting his elbows on his knees.

I didn't wait for him to comment. "I'm trying, Dad. I'm trying because I want Stone in my life."

"That's probably not enough, Camp. You need to want to change because *you* want it. Because you want to be better for you."

I nodded, choked up. Part of me couldn't believe I was even having this conversation. I had half expected him to give me a hard time about everything. Yet, he actually gave me some great ideas and emotional support, even if he didn't like my choices or understand my sexuality. Truly a first. "Thanks." I stood up and leaned over to hug him. I think I hadn't hugged my dad since junior high school.

He stood up and hugged back, but I'd left him utterly speechless.

"Alright. I'm out of your hair, pops."

I left before he had a chance to say anything else. I needed to store this rare interaction in my memory, as the first of its kind. No arguing or fighting. Maybe that was on me, because I honestly wanted to hear what my dad had to say about my future. We didn't get along and we had differing ideas, but I did value his opinion; he happened to be the smartest guy I knew and practically the only one outside of my boss, Andrew, that I considered a real successful, experienced adult.

I waved bye to Kimmy, who was still working and probably had a million things to do. I knew she had long hours, but Karen had already left for the night. Receptionists had better hours. That made me more inclined to want the receptionist's job. *I should write that down like my dad said.* I needed to get a little notebook to carry around so I could note these little epiphanies.

The heat of the day hadn't let go of the city; I walked outside and gulped at the water in the air. The humidity made my hair frizz. I hated that, and I didn't have a ball cap on to hide the mess of blond that desperately needed cut. I ran my hands through it, knowing that would only make it worse. Rounding the corner into the parking garage I was too focused on my hair to see the burly guy leaning against my Beemer, until I was pretty close to him.

"Hey, get off my car," I snarled at him.

The guy stood up straight, smirking at me with his arms crossed over his chest. I recognized him as my dad's angry client from the other day, the one I saw at the restaurant with Julien. I glanced around the garage.

"You really are that bastard's kid, then. Campbell? Campbell Fain?"

I didn't confirm my identity for him. No, I knew something was wrong when a tingling in my gut told me I was in trouble, but the damned van parked beside my BMW confirmed it—gray, dirty, with finger marks trailing through the dirt and a growing web of cracks across the windshield. This guy had been following me for days.

"What do you want?" I asked, although I kind of had it figured out.

"I want that old man of yours to understand what it's like to lose someone they love." He walked toward me, and I took a step back, needing to walk away, but he lunged faster than I could go. I twisted, but he grabbed my waist and arm, pulling me to him.

"If you fight, I'm going to make it hurt." He pronounced his words clearly, distinctly, emphasizing the *hurt* as if it that were the focus of his whole world. If he'd lost someone close, maybe it was, but it didn't stop me from wriggling around, trying to get away.

I remembered hearing one time that you should fight at all cost if someone is trying to take you, because if they take you away from where they'd grab you, they're going to kill you, but they might not do it right away. I would not let this guy torture me to get back at my dad for some perceived wrong. I stomped his foot and lunged with all my body weight. That only brought the big guy down on top of me. He outweighed me by more than fifty pounds. Taller, broader shoulders pushed me down, pinning my chest to the concrete floor.

"Stop fighting," he growled. His beard scratched the back of my neck where my t-shirt ended.

"Help! Fire!" I screamed. Trying to pull more air in my lungs, I gasped and then let out a blood curdling scream. I wasn't above screaming. "Fire!" I screamed again. I'd heard that screaming *fire* would bring help faster than anything else.

Before I could let loose another yell, the guy flipped me to my back and planted his fist in my jaw. I yelled loud at that, but not as loud as I had been and then only animalistic noises came out. My jaw hurt too much to form words. He punched me again. Cold, life-less eyes stared at me from his broad face. The lack of emotion petrified me.

"Shut it!"

"Fuck you!" I groaned out, but it probably sounded more like, "fu-oo," because I couldn't move my jaw. I wanted to scratch the bastard's eyes out, but his knees had my hands pinned. I bucked up, trying to dislodge him.

"No you don't," he said, calmly...too calmly. That scared me more than the grabbing and fighting and even the punches to the jaw. He hit me again with the back of his hand, across the side of my face, between my ear and my eye. I saw stars. Literally. My vision blanked out to black with silvery shiny lights flicking like a million stars. Then the pain settled in. And I had thought my hangover hurt? Hell, that was nothing compared to this new debilitating pain. I tried to touch my sore head, but couldn't move.

The world spun around and my stomach lurched. He picked me up in a fireman's carry, and when his shoulder slammed into my gut, I puked. Right down the motherfucker's back. I squirmed around again, trying to focus on something besides the pain, but it didn't help. He slammed me into the back of the van, seemingly oblivious to my retching.

The air left my lungs and the pit of my stomach turned in on itself.

This was it.

This bastard was going to take me somewhere and kill me. I made a lunge to jump out of the vehicle. I wasn't going anywhere. *Bastard better just fucking kill me now!*

He shoved me back, and when I lunged a second time, his fist connected with the center of my forehead. At least, that's what it felt like. I opened my eyes to a quick flash of him standing over me with a tire iron in his hand before the darkness took me, despite my panic.

16 Stone

Nothing was going to make me feel better. I had on my soft gray sweat pants and my zip-up hoodie, lying sprawled out on my couch. I'd brought my pillow from my bedroom and tried to get comfortable enough to sleep, but it still wasn't coming.

Every time I tried to relax and stop thinking so I could fall asleep, the conversation with Campbell swirled around in my head again. Conversation? No, that wasn't a conversation—more like a slaughter. We'd butchered the thing up completely. I meant to tell Campbell that I wanted to start over, try again, but I'd just dragged the whole mess out and threw it in his face. He obviously hurt over this.

Or maybe not.

Not really knowing what he believed was the worst part. Maybe he hadn't even thought about me in days since he'd left the last message. Maybe, I pushed him too far and maybe he got over it before we'd had that argument at the bar. Maybe I pissed him off, not leaving him alone. I hoped all of that was just my own imagination, hoped he missed me as much as I missed him.

Then I circled back to the fact that I should be pissed off at him. Campbell should have been crawling back to me, begging for another chance. Not the other way around. Maybe I should just leave the whole damned thing alone.

Then again, maybe I'd made it all out to be more dramatic

than it really was. My mom had me questioning everything I thought about Campbell and our so-called relationship. Hell, had I just created all of this in my own imagination? Did Camp even really like me? My gut said that was wrong, but how much of it was wrong?

Ultimately, I just couldn't stop thinking about him. His big haunting eyes, his crazy blond, rebellious hair, and that mile-wide smile that could probably light up the entire city. My heart ached to hear him laugh, just one more time. It was killing me and it had only been two days since I'd seen him last, when we'd fought outside the bar.

I rolled over and smashed my face into the pillow, wishing that it still smelled like him, but it didn't. His musky scent was gone along with the rest of him, leaving me lonely and unsure of myself.

Tossing and turning frustrated me. I sighed and got up. I popped on my Nikes and grabbed my keys, heading out the door. I told myself I was going to get something to eat, just unwind a little. But I didn't head up 22nd to hit McDonalds. I kept traveling west until I hit Channelside and cut over to Nuccio. I didn't know any fast food joints on that side of town.

When I hit Ashley, I turned south, telling myself I wasn't headed over to Bayshore. I wound around back roads until fifteen minutes later I turned down Campbell's street. He lived around the corner from a bakery, but they wouldn't be open at this hour. It was getting late, maybe close to ten at night. I wondered briefly if that was too late to stop in and see if he was home.

There were too many cars in his driveway and lined up on the curb, and the lights were on. None of them were Campbell's Beemer. I passed his house looking for somewhere to park and saw two police cars on the far side of the drive. Police?

My stomach knotted and I parked in front of his neighbor's house. I slammed the door and cut between the cars in the driveway before dashing across the lawn and pounding on the front door.

The tussle-haired poet, Gavin, answered. "Hey, man. They've been trying to find you." He jerked his head for me to follow him in the house. I shut the door quietly behind me and followed him. His roommates were lined up against the breakfast bar, eyeballing me like a felon.

His father sat on the couch next to an older woman with light brown hair, tinged with gray flecks. She sat close to him, crinkling up a tissue in her hands. Her eyes were puffy and red. I figured she must be Campbell's mom, but why were they here? Why was she crying, and why was his father's face stern and scowling like a gargoyle?

Two police officers stood in front of them. One had a little notebook out, jotting things in it. The other looked up at me, trying to keep his features neutral, but his cheek kept flinching, threatening to give him away.

I cleared my throat. "What's going on?"

The officer with the notebook looked up at me. "And who are you, please?"

"Stone Medlock. Where's Campbell?" I turned away to look at the roommate line-up.

Gavin rubbed his face, while the statistics nut picked at his finger nails. I looked at Julien, dressed down for the first time I'd seen. He wore a ratty t-shirt and gray and blue, plaid pajama pants. He stood on one bare foot, with the other foot on top of the first. He opened his mouth to speak, but the officer interrupted him.

"Mr. Medlock. We've been trying to find you for the last few hours. Can you tell me where you've been the last couple of days, particularly around 6 p.m. yesterday evening?" he demanded with authority.

"I got off work at, uh, seven, seven thirty, and went home."

The other cop's hard eyes drilled into me. "Can someone collaborate your story?" He fisted his hands on his hips, legs spread in a confident stance.

"Story?" That pissed me off.

Notebook cop, spoke up. "Sir. We just need to verify

your whereabouts, please."

"Why? What's going on? Where's Campbell?" It was my missing boyfriend, or ex-boyfriend, whose whereabouts mattered to me at the moment.

"We'll explain in a minute. First, please...can anyone verify where you've been?"

"Of course. Lawrence St. James. I work for him."

Notebook cop jotted that down. Everyone in Tampa knew the man. I didn't think I'd get questioned past that, but it didn't stop the cop. "Mr. Medlock, we've been trying to call you for the last few hours. Why haven't you answered the call?"

I pulled my phone out and looked at it. It was off. Again. "It's been turning itself off lately," I grunted, powering back up. "I think I need a new battery."

"Thank you," the other cop answered, but I didn't think he spoke to me. "We'll turn this over to the detectives and get back with you as soon as possible. In the meantime, please call us if anything else happens, especially if you're contacted."

Campbell's father stood and shook the cop's hand. I stared at my phone. Fifteen missed calls from Campbell. Apparently, the cops had Campbell's phone and were calling me. So, where the hell was Campbell?

The cops left and I looked at Julien again.

He crossed his arms, his red eyes stared back at me and he cleared his throat. "He's missing. We think he's been kidnapped."

"What?"

Before I could answer, Campbell's dad came back in the living room, followed by a lovely young woman with thick dark hair pulled back into a pony tail. Her green eyes flashed like emeralds in the sun as she looked over the room. "It's too late to get anything going. The labs will be analyzing the blood and uh, other samples, and fingerprints off his car first thing tomorrow. I called in a few favors and I asked Sandefer to check on things. For tonight that's the best I can do." She sat next to Campbell's mother and clasped the older woman's hands.

Mitchell Fain turned to look at me. "He told me about you. Before... He told me..."

I'd never seen a man his age break down. "What?"

The green-eyed beauty who seemed to be directing the investigation looked up. "Are you Stone?"

I nodded. She seemed to have her shit together, despite wearing yoga pants and a giant t-shirt with *Don't talk to me until I have my coffee* written on the front in bold letters.

"I'm Lorain Montgomery. Family friend." She stood up and held her hand out for me to shake.

I shook her hand, surprised at her firm grip.

"I don't know how much Camp has told you about me, but we've been friends," she nodded at Julien, then continued, "the three of us. Since we were kids."

I shrugged; I knew who she was. "What happened?"

Lorain sat back down, but as the obvious spokesperson, she finally told me. "He left his father's office yesterday, around six and no one has seen him since. They found blood." She swallowed hard. "And vomit. In the parking lot, next to his car. His phone was on the ground a few feet away."

"Why? Why would someone want to...?" I couldn't finish my sentence. Hurting Campbell? I wanted to kill someone right then.

"We don't know." Lorain gave her head a little shake and stared off into the distance, as if looking at nothing. Her eyes glazed over.

My leg bounced with nervous energy. This couldn't be happening. "What can I do?"

"Nothing," Mitchell said, putting his big hand on my shoulder. He was a hefty guy, much bigger boned than Campbell's delicate frame. His mother had a bit of weight on her, but it was obvious he'd inherited his stature from her. She easily could have been a tiny, blonde beauty just like Campbell in her day. She obviously loved her son very much, as she was beyond distraught.

Gavin appeared almost mysteriously at my side and

handed me a big, black mug. "Coffee, dude," he said softly. I took the mug and sipped it. Although black, it tasted slightly sweet. I could deal with that. Maybe I couldn't deal with anything else at the moment. I still hadn't wrapped my head around things. Where was my Campbell?

"Listen, Stone..." Mitchell spoke up, looking at me with a soft expression. "Campbell said he cared for you very much. You have to understand. Most of his adult life has been about rebelling against me and what I wanted for him. You kind of got caught up in that. If...If..." He grumbled under his breath. I didn't hear what he said, but it sounded like a curse. "When we get him back. Please. Give him another chance."

I nodded. "That's not ever been in question. He's everything to me." I didn't know what made me say those words. Why didn't I ever say them to Campbell? I could have had him in my arms, safe, instead of out in the world, vulnerable. "He should have been with me." My voice broke on the last words.

Lorain stood up and crossed the living room, throwing her arms around me. "No. Don't. This is not your fault. Not anybody's fault. Except whoever did this," she said to the whole room before whispering in my ear, "We'll get him back."

I didn't know if I believed her. I wanted to, but when people disappeared like that... I couldn't finish my thought. Wouldn't. I had to have one more chance with Campbell. I just had to.

Mrs. Fain cried with loud sobs that drug Lorain's attention back to her. The two women sat together on the couch with Lorain's arms around Mrs. Fain, comforting the best she could. Mrs. Fain mumbled through her tears, but none of it sounded coherent.

A part of me refused to believe any of this. I sipped from my mug, wondering what else could happen.

Mr. Fain cleared his throat. "When he didn't show up at home, Jay-Jay called around. That's when we found his car and called the police."

"Okay."

"Nothing we can do now but wait." I wasn't sure if he spoke to me, the others, or himself.

17 Campbell

The pain in my face woke me up with a throbbing alarm. I cracked my eyes open, but immediately shut them again because it just fucking hurt. From the first waking moment, I considered I'd really tied one on with this massive hangover, making my head feel like it had been hit with a tire iron. Then I remembered a little of what had really happened, thinking I might have actually been hit with a tire iron.

I groaned through my agony and tried to roll over. Something heavy pulled at my arms and I heard metal scraping metal. With another painful eye opening I saw chains scraping against the metal frame of the bed I lay on. It had a thin mattress, like a futon. And chains—around my wrists. That realization scared the crap out of me. The big guy had me chained up on a bed, helpless. My body jerked with spasms and I curled up in a tight ball to get a grip, but I couldn't stop shaking. I shook so badly my teeth chattered, banging together like something from a horror movie.

I'd been so concerned with my face and the shivering that I didn't hear him come in. He placed a big hand on my shoulder. "Randy? You okay?"

I didn't answer, just kept chattering and shaking.

"Hang on, babe. I got you." His soft and comforting voice jarred my senses. "Here, Randy." He covered me with a blanket and sat at the edge of the mattress, rubbing my back and shoulder. "This will warm you up." He didn't touch me in an intimate way, but he didn't have to. Caring for me and calling me some other name like something right out of Psycho had my nerves fraying. Norman Bates here had obviously lost a few marbles, which made my situation that much worse.

Despite my fear, my body relaxed and warmed up and my brain churned, thinking in proportion with the added heat. Until I tried to move again. Pain lanced through my head, searing pain like someone had attacked my brain with a cheese grater. "Gah," I moaned out and tried to bring my hands to my head, but they wouldn't budge.

"You need Tylenol or something?"

I tried to answer with a "Yes," but it came out as nothing more than a croak and a hiss. I guess it was enough for Norman to get up and search through a bunch of shit piled in the corner. I could see a big green duffle bag, some paper sacks, and a plastic case that looked a lot like fishing tackle.

"Ah, here." He came back to the futon with a handful of pills and a bottle of water. "Can you sit up?"

Right. I could barely move.

Norman sat the water down. "Here." He put the pills in my hand and closed my fingers around them before gently, but firmly, grabbing my shoulders and hefting me up. That gave me a better look at the chains he'd bound me with. I had leather cuffs locked on each wrist. A chain looped down from each cuff to a huge cement block, through the hole on the block, and back up to the wrist. I could move around enough, but I'd have to lug that cement block everywhere I went, plus the chains were a little heavy, too. They weren't big huge truck-pulling chains, but they weren't thin, easily broken ones either. This guy had thought things out, mostly.

I feared taking the pills. What if they weren't Tylenol, but Roofies or something? I popped them in my mouth anyway. Hell, if he wanted to rape me, he could do that without drugging me. I swallowed the water down, pulling in half the bottle. "Ice," I moaned out as I finished.

Norman stared at me, as if seeing me for the first time and grumbled something under his breath.

I gritted the words out, through my teeth, barely opening my mouth. "Please. Ice. For my face." I wanted to take advantage of his caring mood before it left.

"I didn't think about that. Sorry, you'll have to wait." His eyes took in my face, shoulders, and chest. "You don't look like your dad."

"No. My mom." I kept my answers short, mostly because it hurt like hell to talk. I wondered if he broke my jaw. "Why?" I croaked out and then drank down the rest of the water before he had time to change his mind about it.

"Why? Why anything. The justice of the mind is sometimes more important than the guys in charge, the so-called officials. They tell you. You know how it is. Randy was my partner, my life. They took...all of it, my love, my life. That's it. We have to fight back or it's for nothing and I'm nothing. Understand?"

I tried to shake my head to tell him I had no idea what the fuck he was talking about, but it hurt too much and I just kind of groaned.

"It's okay. Get some more rest and I'll go get ice and food."

I laid back on the futon and looked at the rafters soaring above me as I listened to Norman jingling his car keys and the clicks of the locks on whatever door he'd bound. The roof had to be thirty feet up and, along with the walls, looked like corrugated tin. The ceiling curved slightly inward with long metal structures crossing above me. A few high windows lined one side of the huge open room. The other side, the one Norman left out of, had a regular sized door off center and what looked like a huge sliding door next to it. That one was big enough for large trucks to pass through. Or aircraft.

That's when I realized some of the roaring noise in my head had to be jet engines and not my injury. We were close to the airport. Probably only ten to twenty minutes from my dad's office on Westshore. I didn't know how any of that would help me, but I'd use it if I could, since I was fairly certain that good old Norman Bates was going to kill me, despite the Tylenol and the blanket.

I had managed to calm myself a lot, but as soon as the crunching of keys in the lock echoed through the hangar my body involuntarily trembled. I expected the psycho to kill me at any time, and I'd never even really apologized to Stone. I wanted to tell him I loved him. I wanted to shake my dad's hand and give him a hug. I wanted to kiss my mom and take Lorain out to dinner and just hang out with her and Julien. I wanted to tell Gavin that he didn't screw things up for me with Stone and I didn't blame him.

Norman Bates walked in and I got a really good look at him. He had big, burly shoulders and a beard, a little messier than I remembered. His eyes held more of a sadness than the ice-cold intensity I thought I'd seen earlier. He marched across the cement floor like a boss.

Aside from the futon and pile of bags, I couldn't see much of anything else in the hangar. Maybe some old, rusty airplane parts stacked in the very back. Nothing that looked like I could use as a weapon, even if I could make my way all the way across the room, carrying a cement block, before Norman could catch me. Right.

He handed me a burger wrapped up in yellowish McDonald's paper. "I don't think I can eat yet." Chewing and swallowing hard food was not an option. I could barely move my jaw enough to even talk.

"Okay. I got ice." He held out a McDonald's large drink cup, white and waxy and imprinted with the golden arches. I took it from him. It had just ice inside. I pressed it against my cheek where the worst of the pain throbbed. "Better?"

"Guess...so what next?"

He shrugged. "Your father is a... he's bad. He's done bad things and he needs to understand what it feels like to lose someone he loves."

My eyes grew wide. Yep. He was going to kill me. I didn't know how to deal with someone that had just jumped off the rails. "I know he's a dick. But, God...man...I didn't do anything. I'm just a kid."

He stared at me from beneath bushy eyebrows. "You're small. But you're grown. You're not a kid."

I held my empty hand up, as if to give him a good *what the fuck?*

"You have a job. Friends. A nice car. A house. If you didn't earn all of that on your own, then you're as bad as he is, as bad as the oppressors. Do you want that? Does that make you just a kid?"

"No, look. I didn't do anything to you. I don't even know who you are." That was about the extent of my pleading. Despite the ice, my jaw pulsated with nearly blinding pain. I closed my eyes, praying to see my family and friends one more time. To see Stone one more time.

"It's okay, Randy. I'll save this for later." He packed up the burgers and stuffed them in the white sack.

I wanted to ask him more about Randy and what had happened to push him to actually act out this bizarre scheme, but I also didn't want to say anything that might set him off. I had no idea who I was dealing with.

After he had everything packed up, he turned to me again, his eyes examining me as if looking for some answer that I didn't have. "My name's Kris. With a K. Your dad would know that."

"Client?"

Kris nodded. At least I had a real name, instead of Norman, to call him, though if the crazy shoe fits...

He sat on the edge of the mattress and put his big paw on my thigh, making me jump. "I'm not going to hurt you Campbell. As long as you don't fight anymore. Man, you fought like a wildcat." He put his thick finger in my face. "I didn't mean to hurt you, but you just wouldn't give up."

Had he expected me to come quietly? Fuck that.

"So, just relax. Keep the ice on. I'll help you to the bathroom in a few minutes. I have to scope out the place first. In everything, you have to keep your defenses up. Everything. You never know when the oppressors are going to come at you, dude. They can be very subtle, you know."

I nodded. I had no idea what he was talking about. Was he slipping in and out of reality or just making me think he was nuts?

I watched silently as he roamed the hangar. Some of the time he walked back and forth, pacing, and some of the time he seemed to be looking for something. At one point he put his head against the wall, as if listening to what may or may not be going on outside the hangar. He mumbled under his breath the entire time. I had no idea what he said but I wasn't going to interrupt his antics to ask, either.

The minutes ticked by. My cup of ice melted and I took another Tylenol, drinking more water. I stretched out as best I could on the mattress, wrapped up in the dirty blanket. I wanted to go to sleep and wake up in my own bed, or better yet, in Stone's bed. If I let myself believe that would never happen again, I might not make it out of the hangar alive. I wouldn't let my mind go down that road, the one where Kris with a K slit my throat after raping and beating me. I expected him to torture me for my dad's secret client information. Perhaps I knew something useful about the oppressors he kept muttering about. I had no idea, and I didn't want to know. I closed my eyes, willing my restless brain to stop churning.

As soon as I drifted off, Kris banged his leg against the bed. "Hey. Camp! That's you right? Campbell Fain? Your friends call you Camp?"

I opened my eyes. "Yeah."

"Okay. You need a bathroom break? Now's the time. Take it or leave it. In the hospital they give you a pan or stick a tube up your dick. I don't have any of those things. Just a little piss pot over there." He pointed across the room.

"'Kay."

He picked up the block and led me to the door. Inside

was a toilet and a sink with an old cloudy mirror. I peered in it, despite its lack of reflection in the dim room with the only light coming in from a dirty window high up the wall. My face looked red and blue and purple. Some spots around the edges were yellowing and some even looked green. The entire side of my face could have been an abstract painting of pain. *Mother fucker!*

I took a quick piss and wiped my hands on my jeans—thankful for the millionth time that I could wear jeans to work—not even bothering to turn the rusty knobs of the sink. When I opened the door, Kris grabbed the cement block and walked me back to the futon.

"Healthcare is full of oppressors," Kris said softly, sitting next to me again. "There's enough without your dad making it worse. Him and that blasphemous organization that helped him. Paid him."

"What?"

He stared at me, grabbed my shoulder. "You didn't know?" His face screamed serious. He believed what he said about my father, but I still didn't understand him.

"Know what?"

"The hospital was at fault. It was their fault Randy died. Their mother fucking fault. They did everything wrong. Took my lover from me. His doctor, the staff, and that fucking Patient Safety Organizations. All infiltrated by oppressors and they paid your dad." He pointed at me. "Paid him a lot more than I ever could have won in the courts." He backed off and hung his head. He grumbled under his breath, something about the oppressors again, but I couldn't tell what he said. I was still hung up on his initial accusation.

"Kris? Kris?" Finally, he looked up at me. That stark sadness sat in his eyes again. "Are you saying someone paid my dad to throw your case? Is that what you're saying?"

"Yes. Of course. I understand why, but it doesn't matter. Mitchell Fain still must pay. The oppressors cannot win this. No."

"W…Wait." I held my hand up, jingling the attached

chain.

"Listen, it's okay. Randy had to go. God sent the demons to the earth to define and control." He stood up and paced back and forth, throwing his hands in the air. "The Bible tells us so, right? It says in black and white. For thousands of years. Blood and sweat and death. That's all that they bring. But, no! God loves his children. I think it could have been aliens. What if the demons were really aliens? They could still be here, cast to Earth. But that sounds crazy, right?"

I shook my head, and sucked my lip into my mouth, regretting that instantly as the sharp pain from where the cut on my lip stung.

"It doesn't matter. Fuck! Nothing matters!" he yelled, his voice echoing through the vast, empty space of the hangar. "Sometimes I want to just punch God in the face."

My heart leapt to my throat. Surely I'd run out of time. Kris yelled, cursed, paced the floor, stomped his feet, and I thought I might puke; my stomach churned just watching him, listening to him. I wiped the sweat off my forehead with the blanket and pulled it over my shoulders and closed my eyes, trying to tune out Kris's rant and wishing I could make myself invisible.

18 Stone

I ran my hand through my hair, pulling at my curls. It was some indeterminate time after midnight. My eyes stung and I sipped on cinnamon spiked coffee. There was no way I could sleep until Campbell came home. The tough lawyer chick had long since left and Campbell's folks had crashed in Campbell's room. Honestly, it bothered me. I wanted to be the one snuggling in his bed and holding his pillow with his scent on it for comfort, cold as it would be.

Leaning against the breakfast bar, I watched Tony and Julien playing Xbox. They weren't into it though, just trying to pass time. They didn't call out, no laughing, no animation—just two lugs going through motions. It tugged at something in my chest, physically aching. I needed my tiger back, needed his laughter.

"Hey," Gavin startled me out of my sad musings.

"Huh, what?"

"I'm sorry."

What in the world he was sorry for, I didn't know and didn't care. I took a sip of coffee, ignoring whatever he had to say. None of it mattered. I only cared about finding Campbell and bringing him home.

"Go home. Or crash on the couch. Or something."

Pushing the coffee across the bar, I cringed. "I can't. I have to...I have to do something. Feel like I should be combing the streets or something."

"You can't do anything but wait with the rest of us. The police have the best shot at this...and hey! His dad is kind of a big wig around here. Right? They're going to be on it."

Julien walked up next to them, the game obviously abandoned. "Hey! Lorain is going to be all over their asses too. Nobody wants that. Believe me!"

I wanted to laugh and might have, but that thing inside me, that allowed me to laugh, was broken. I huffed, "I get it. I really do. It just doesn't make me feel any better."

Gavin grabbed my mug to give it a top-off and Julien put his arm around me. "Listen," he said quietly. "I know you weren't together long, but you were better for him than anyone...ever."

I gracefully accepted the mug back and sipped it, willing my emotions to stop overwhelming me. My stinging eyes wanted to tear up and the lump in my throat refused to go down. So I sat on the bar stool with Julien standing next to me and Gavin standing on the kitchen-side of the bar, both watching me. What were they waiting for? I gulped at my coffee. This wasn't some damn funeral. He hadn't died already. "Don't they say the first forty-eight hours are crucial? If they don't find him in that window—"

"No. Not true," Julien grumbled, letting his arm slide off my shoulder.

"Besides," Gavin added. "They're going to find him. Quickly." It was nothing but an empty promise. He didn't know that. He didn't know anything.

"I feel like I need to do something," I repeated.

Julien put his arm over my shoulder again and gripped tight before releasing me and going back into the living room to sit on the floor beside Tony and turn their game back up. Gavin poured himself another cup and then started another pot. The sounds around me were muted. The world around me had gone gray. No light, no sound...without Campbell I could only see a bleak existence.

I just wanted to tell him I could forgive him and get over it, all of it. With him missing, I realized quickly that we could work through anything, even his lies. They weren't life or death; he hadn't cheated on me. It had been a short time, but I already knew I loved him. I wanted him back. Giving up on reinforcing my walls, I let the tears fall cold down my face.

19 Campbell

The sun streaming through the high windows jolted me awake. My arm tingled numbly where I'd been lying on it, but the tingling that started up with all the pins and needles was nothing compared to the throbbing of my face. I groaned loudly.

Kris had left me here sometime the night before and when I was sure he was gone, I'd screamed. No one came, and I ended up with a sore throat on top of everything else.

I'd tried to throw shit I found around the hangar at the windows: a wrench, a box of nails, a few loose bolts. It didn't help. I tried to maneuver myself to get out of a window. I tried to pick the lock on the door. None of it worked.

My arms and legs were sore from lugging the cement block around, but that still didn't take away from the agonizing hurt pulsing down my face. I still could barely eat. I just knew the asshole had broken my jaw.

Groaning, I stretched out across the futon. Fucking miserable. I cried, not trying to hold it back at all. I cried like I hadn't done since I was seven and got hit in the face by a wayward baseball. I wanted to go to the bathroom, take a piss, and wash my face. I wanted to find the Tylenol. I wanted to go home. Exhausted from already lugging the block around, I knew none of that was happening, not any time soon, if ever.

I heard the door unlocking and opening, but I didn't stop crying and my nose ran, snotting down my face and turning me into a sniveling mess.

"Hey, hey," Kris said, cooing softly. I hated him.

He tried to wipe my face and I shrank away from him. He grabbed my ankle, it didn't hurt, but I kicked at him with my other foot anyway, catching him in the side of the head. When he drew his arm back to punch me, I curled up into the fetal position and sobbed. He didn't punch me.

"I'm sorry. Man, Campbell. I didn't mean to hurt you. Shit."

A minute later he dropped a wet cloth on my hip. I wiped my face, the cool rag soothing the bruises. I sat up and blew my nose into the rag. *Fuck him if he had to clean it!* I dropped it on the floor and stared up at him. His dark eyes twinkled, but didn't give away whatever he thought or felt. "Why?"

He dropped an orange prescription bottle and a bottle of water on the futon beside me. "This is Tramadol. Stronger than the Tylenol, but still won't make you loopy."

"Why?" I asked him again.

"Because I meant it. I didn't mean to hurt you. You're just collateral damage, but I still feel bad about it. Look, I got egg drop soup, too. Full of protein and easier for you to eat."

"No, I mean why are you doing this? Just let me go."

Kris wrung his hands together and turned in circles. I ignored him, going for the soup. My stomach growled, it knew food was coming, but not fast enough.

"I need to go to the bathroom," I said after a few bites.

Kris stopped pacing and looked at me, as if I'd just told him aliens had landed; although, in his head, maybe that wouldn't be all that strange.

I huffed. *Fuck him anyway!* "This block is heavy and I'm fucking sore all over. Just fucking help me."

"Oh! Sorry."

After the trip to the bathroom, Kris planted me back on the futon, and I slowly ate the soup while he paced. "What are you going to do anyway? Eventually, they'll find me. What exactly do you hope to accomplish?"

"The oppressors cannot get away with this. I told you.

They disregarded Randy completely. It's not right. They need to know they can't treat people like this."

Back to that. "There's got to be a better way. What do I have to do with any of it?"

"You're like Randy. You're a victim."

I didn't know anything about Randy or Kris and his madness, but I'd never seen myself as a victim, even now. "Fuck you!" I sat the empty plastic container on the ground and leaned back against the mattress. I had to figure out how to get out of here.

"I'm sorry," Kris murmured under his breath.

"It's not going to work," I scoffed. "My dad hates me. He probably doesn't even know I'm missing."

"Oh, he knows!"

"He doesn't care," I stated the simple fact. I'd only just begun questioning my father and his motivations, but now I didn't want to examine that. It wouldn't matter. I stared up at the rafters. The bright sun sneaking through the dirty windows illuminated particles floating through the air; what they were and why we couldn't see them unless the sun filtered against them in that certain way?

"He knows. He cares. He's learning his lesson," Kris burbled, getting louder and louder. "He cannot play with the powers that be without getting burned. The oppressors can't win. They can't. They were sent here by God, cast down from the heavens, but they still have rules to follow."

I let the tears stream from the corner of my eyes. "You're going to kill me, aren't you?"

Kris didn't pay a damn bit of attention to me. He paced and rambled senselessly to himself about demons and heaven and God and the devil.

Something insane bubbled up from inside me and laughter exploded my from my gut as well as my mouth. I was losing it. This had to be the way my life ended. Kidnapped and killed to teach my father that he couldn't disregard people. *How fucking ironic?*

As I lay there, laughing hysterically, watching the air

particles dance through the rafters and Kris's jumbled words joining them, I realized that I regretted losing Stone more than anything else. I hadn't allowed myself to really try with him. I'd given up, repeatedly. I'd lied. I'd hid. I couldn't face the fact that this adorable man could actually want me—for me and not who my father was.

My heart ached for him more than anything. I swore to myself that I would try. If I made it out of this broken down airplane hangar alive, I would try to get Stone back and I wouldn't give up and I wouldn't lie and I would...I would tell him I loved him.

20 Stone

Sleep finally took me, but not for long. I jumped straight up off the couch where I'd crashed when the banging on the door roused the house.

"Hey! Everybody! We have news!" Lorain pushed her way past two guys wearing plain suits, one brown and one dark blue. They both had their sleeves pushed up and their color coordinated ties pulled down. "These are the detectives leading Campbell's case." The suits nodded as everyone gathered in the living room.

All the roommates lined the breakfast bar, except Julien, who went in the kitchen and got another pot of coffee going. The Fains came in and perched on the edge of the couch, hands clasped together at their knees. I stood in the middle of the room for a moment, then moved off to the side to give the detectives room.

"Coffee?" Julien called from the kitchen, but everyone ignored him.

"So," the detective in the brown suit spoke up. "The blood definitely belonged to Campbell. We need all of you to get fingerprinted today so we can tell which prints are unaccounted for. That's easier and faster than running every print we lifted off the car."

"But that's not the best news, and only a formality," Lorain piped in. "Tell them." She motioned in the air for the detectives to get on with it.

"We pulled the security footage and we have a good idea of who did this. We also found the vehicle and tailed it this morning, so we think we know where he's holding Campbell."

Blue suit spoke up. "We need Mr. Fain to come to the station with us and identify the suspect. We'll also have some other questions for you." He looked at Mitchell Fain.

Lorain spoke up. "That's all formalities. They know where he is and within the hour a S.W.A.T. team will be going in to rescue him. So, he'll be home by the end of the day."

"Given that he doesn't need extensive medical treatment. Please, Lorain. He's going straight to the hospital, so don't get your hopes up," Brown suit finished. Once he'd finished, he gazed at Lorain with pretty blue eyes and she smiled sweetly at him. They obviously liked each other, making me feel a lot better about her being around. I'd been jealous of her, just from what Campbell had told me about her and his expectations of her, making her presence uncomfortable for me. The glances she shared with the detective helped; they were obviously into each other.

"Campbell's coming home?" Mrs. Fain stood up and grabbed Lorain's hands.

"Yes. Soon."

"You sure he's okay?" Julien joined me in the living room with raised eyebrows and handed me a cup of coffee. I took it without comment, and joined him in staring down the blue suit.

"No. We aren't sure of anything at this point. Ms. Montgomery is being optimistic."

"We're pretty sure, though. I mean, there wasn't as much blood as we originally thought. Not enough to suspect a lot of trauma. And this guy led them right to the place."

"We don't know that for sure, either. They'll send scouts in ahead of time and if it looks like he's there and we can get him out, the S.W.A.T. team will retrieve him."

"Okay," Julien said, staring into his coffee mug.

I cleared my throat. "So, what? We just wait now?"

"Yes. Go get your fingerprints done. It'll give you

something to do."

Gavin walked in and bumped his shoulder against mine, gently. "Is that absolutely necessary to do now? Today?"

The brown suit sighed. "No. Sometime this week is fine. Since we're pretty sure who this guy is, it's not a big deal. But Mr. Fain, you will need to come with us, now. We need to confirm the identification."

Campbell's dad stood up. He'd been too quiet. "Why?"

"I don't understand." Mrs. Fain sat back down on the couch, ringing her hands.

Lorain narrowed her eyes at him, making me wonder what she knew that she wasn't telling. "He's one of your clients."

"Oh." He didn't comment further or ask which one, leaving the rest of us to wonder, but Lorain slid a shifty look at him as he quickly left with the detectives. Mrs. Fain walked out behind them.

Apparently, Julien noticed too and as soon as the front door closed, he confronted her. "So, what gives Lorain? What aren't you saying?"

She fisted her hands on her hips and bit at her lower lip. "I can't say yet. Just...let it go for now, Jay-Jay."

"Fine, but I saw how you were looking at Mr. Fain. If it's something about him, Camp should know, and you'd better not hold back on him." He pointed at her. "You can't always play peace maker. You're not Switzerland. Pick a side. The right side."

"I'm always on Camp's side. Shesh...let's just get cleaned up and go over to the hospital. They'll probably take him to St. Joseph's by the stadium."

With a plan in hand, everyone else moved with purpose, but I dragged myself up, sluggish. My feet didn't want to move. I think my heart stayed behind, there in the living room, open and empty.

Gavin finally got me rolling. "Dude," he said with a shove. "He really will want to see you. More than the rest of our ugly mugs for sure." It wasn't his words, though, but the look in his eyes as he said them that had me moving. That misty gray gaze seemed to say that he knew how much I cared for Campbell and that he knew Campbell cared as well. How much would any of it matter in the end? I didn't know, but I needed to be there for Campbell. I needed to be supportive for me as much as for him, so I moved.

"Okay. Sure. I'm going home to shower and change. I'll meet y'all there. 'Kay?"

"Yeah, sure man." Gavin put his hand on my shoulder and gave it a little shake. "It's going to be fine."

I didn't know if he believed that for sure or not, but I had to hold on to that. The police team knew what they were doing and they'd get Campbell out as safely as possible.

Julien stopped us just as I headed out behind Lorain. "Hey, Lorain! Wait up."

"What?" She stopped and turned, pinning me to the wall in the front hallway.

"Camp and I were out the other day and this guy was at the restaurant, staring at Camp and he looked out of place. Rumpled clothes, unkempt a little. Camp said he was one of his dad's clients. One that wasn't happy with his service and had showed his ass in the office. Is that? You think it may be the same guy?"

"Maybe. Why the hell didn't you say anything before?"

"I just thought of it." He shrugged.

"Well. Won't do us much good right now, but later. Tomorrow, maybe. You can go in and pick him out of a lineup or something. Might at least build the case against him, if you're right."

"Yeah, that'd make me feel better."

Lorain rolled her eyes, very unprofessionally, but she was more than just their lawyer, they'd grown up together. A fact I was all too well aware of. "Come on, Stone. Forget these clowns." She grabbed my arm, pulling me out to the driveway.

I gave Julien a quick wave and headed out to my car. I opened the door, but before I could get in, Lorain tapped the top of my car to get my attention. She glared at me over the roof. "What?"

"Whatever happened between you two, just forget it and move on."

"What's that mean?"

"You're good for him. He needs you. So whatever stupid-shit fucked up thing he did? He did for good reason. I know, because I know him. So forgive him, forget it and get on with it because, like I said, he needs you."

I'd wondered how she felt about it all. I wondered what they'd all believed, especially his parents and Julien and her—those that were closest to him. I'd been foisted on them at this point, but no one had pushed me away. "I'm here. I'm going to the hospital. Don't you think that means something?"

"I'm a lawyer. I often fail to believe initial impressions. It takes more than that to earn my trust."

"Okay."

She tapped on the roof of my car again. "See you there."

Mrs. Fain walked back up the driveway, apparently not leaving with the detectives and her husband. She looked a little lost or confused and I wondered how much of this she was really processing.

Lorain sighed and rubbed her temples. "I have to take his mom home first, so it'll be near an hour before I'm there. Don't let anyone run you off." She pointed at me with a hard glare. She looked and sounded severe with her pony tail making her face seem harsh and her no gruff, nonsense voice. But just for that instant, I could tell she had a big heart. My jealousy slipped away. Campbell needed people close to him and that included Lorain.

I got in the car with the first real smile I'd had in nearly two weeks. With luck, I'd see Campbell home and healthy by the end of the day. That's what mattered most.

21 Campbell

There was nothing to do but sleep, yet I woke up every time I rolled over on my face. The Tramadol pills helped, but lying on the bruises trumped those suckers. I had no idea I slept on my face so much. Amazing what you find out about yourself when you've been kidnapped and beaten.

Kris only left to pick up food, otherwise he'd pace the floors, making me nervous. I tried to keep quiet. His attention was never good and I kind of hoped he'd forgotten about me most of the time. Feeling better from the sleep, the Tramadol, and the soup, I picked up the block myself to go to the bathroom while Kris rambled around on the far side of the hangar, pacing and talking to himself.

I looked around the bathroom again after taking a long piss. I could probably climb up and get out of the window if I could get out of the chains. I fingered the leather cuffs. They were comfortable, not chaffing at all, but the leather, though soft, was also thick. Ripping them off would be impossible. They were snug enough that I couldn't slip my hands out of them either—I was no fucking Houdini. I could try to pick the tiny locks that kept them buckled on, but I didn't have any tools to pick them with. I made a mental note to search the debris in the back of the hangar the next time Kris went out. Maybe I could find a little screwdriver, a small nail, or something.

A loud banging on the door made me jump. "Come on.

You have to be done pissing."

"Let me wash my fucking hands," I grumbled turning on the water. He banged on the door again, making me think he'd come in and drag me back to the futon. My hands trembled under the slightly rusty water. I had to get out of there, had to try and talk him into letting me go.

I opened the door just as he'd lifted his fist to bang on it again, surprising him. "I'm done."

He grunted and grabbed the cement block, following me back to the futon with it. He dropped it beside the mattress and stared at me when I sat down. "Look. I really don't—"

"I get it," I interrupted him. "Really. I told you how I feel about dear old dad. Hey! Maybe I can help you." I didn't want to help him with anything, but he sure as hell didn't need to know that. "If you let me go, I can get inside my dad's office for you. I can find out things. You know, like a spy?"

"I'm not letting you go. At least not yet."

I huffed. "Why not? This isn't working for you."

"I...I just. Look. Randy was everything to me. My whole world. He's gone and the case is closed. Nothing matters now. If I end up dead...that's just great. I'll be with Randy again." For a second, I thought he was going to cry, but he didn't. His body shook and his breathing labored.

"What happened?" I tried to get him to focus. "Kris."

"I...I...Randy was. I am..." His breathing changed, coming faster, almost panting. He rubbed his hands along his jeans. "He was...Oh God, the love of my life...I'm alone..." He gasped, as if he couldn't get enough air in his lungs.

"Dude. Kris. Are you okay?" I reached out for his shoulder and the chain dragged over his thigh.

"No...N...No. Can't..."

"Take long slow breaths. Kris. Come on. Breathe in slowly." For a minute, I wondered why I was trying to help him. If he passed out, maybe I could find the keys in his pockets and get the hell out of there. Something deep inside me clicked, changed, seeing him like this, like a victim. That's how he saw himself, my dad's victim. He saw me as a victim too, because he saw himself that way. I wondered how many other victims my dad had.

"Come on. Kris. Relax. Breathe in slowly." I rubbed his shoulder, despite the clinking chains.

In a minute, he calmed down. "Sorry. Sorry. Just...a panic attack. Happens now and then."

"Kris. It's okay. You're under a lot of stress. It'd probably help if you let me go. I'll help you. I promise. This isn't going to end well for you at all, but I can help."

He smiled shyly and raised just his eyes to look at me through his bangs. "You're nice. I believe you would help me, but it's too late. Really. I'm glad you're not like your dad."

"Okay. Me too. Just don't kill me, okay."

He shook his head. "No, no. I'm not."

Loud banging echoed through the hangar, drawing Kris's attention and mine as well. "What'd you do?" he yelled and shoved me backwards on the mattress. My heart raced and leapt like a freaking horse at a fox hunt.

Voices from outside carried inside. Some I couldn't understand, but I heard Kris's name and mine, but it only freaked him out more. He leaned over me, letting his weight push me into the mattress. His huge hands circled my throat, but he wasn't squeezing. Yet.

"What did you do? I'm going to fucking kill you, you little shit. You called them. Brought them here. Brought the oppressors."

"I didn't. Please." I was not above begging—at all.

He dragged me to the floor. My arm scraped across the cement block and my head banged on the concrete floor. That was going to help my concussion for sure. "Shh, be quiet. Don't make me kill you, Campbell."

"Kris, Kris, please. I didn't do anything. Please. I never got a chance to apologize to him to tell him that I loved him. Please, don't do this."

"Who? Your father? Your fucking father? The oppressor!" he screamed at me, spittle flying in my face.

"No. Not him. Stone. My boyfriend. Please." I could

barely hear myself for the commotion going on. It sounded like a battering ram pounding on the door. I hoped they would hurry, because Kris's fingers tightened around my throat and I didn't put him killing me with his bare hands out of the realm of possibilities for the day.

"Well, damn," he said softly, but he didn't remove his hands and his weight pressed on my stomach and chest making it harder and harder to breathe.

I covered his hands with mine and looked him in his stormy eyes, begging with all I had, thinking of Stone, and I asked him one more time. "Please?"

My air cut off.

I could feel my pulse beating in my temples.

I closed my eyes and pictured Stone's face and ever-changing eyes shining down at me with love.

The love I lost.

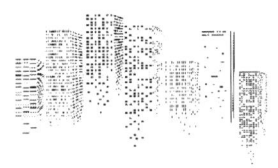

The door screeched and the bang of metal hitting concrete reverberated through the hangar. "Kristofer Turner! Put your hands up where we can see them. You're under arrest for kidnapping, assault and battery, and anything else we think of to throw at you."

Slowly, he let go of my throat.

"Do it. Please?" I rasped. My throat stung where he'd pushed on it.

He gave me a subtle nod and stood up, putting his hands in the air. Pure sorrow melted over his face. He wasn't thinking about getting arrested; he was thinking of Randy and maybe of me.

A cop dressed in riot gear came behind him and wrenched his arms behind his back, reading the Miranda Rights and cuffing him.

"Do that, Camp," he said looking at me and giving me a

curt nod. "Tell him before it's too late. Before you don't get another chance."

"Shut up!" the cop said. "Did you not hear the *used against you* part?" He pulled Kris away and I cried, sobbing and shaking. I was slightly hysterical but it didn't really matter. I was going to live. I was going to be able to see Stone at least one more time.

Strong arms surrounded me, lifted me up. "Mr. Fain. Are you hurt?"

"God yes," I moaned, giving in to the safety of the police.

"Okay. Paramedics will be here in just a moment. They'll take you to the hospital. Your family is already there. Okay?"

"Yes." I barely understood what he'd said, but it didn't matter. These guys were my fucking heroes. They'd rescued me and I no longer had to be strong. Everything that had happened since Kris attacked me in the parking lot came down on me at once, turning me into a puddle of mess and goo and tears and snot.

The cop didn't let go of me until I lay on a stretcher, moving outside the hangar and into an ambulance, leaving the nightmare behind.

22 Stone

When I got home there was a package sitting by my front door. I hadn't ordered anything, so I had no idea what it could be. I picked it up and carried it into the house, dropped it on the couch, and went to shower and change. Getting back to Campbell was my number one priority. Yet, after putting on clean clothes, my curiosity got the better of me and I took a closer look.

An online gift store label graced the front of the package. I used my house key to bust the tape and open it up. It had snacks and games and a card.

Stone,

I miss you and I'm thinking of you. I'm hoping we can enjoy this together. Please.

Love,

Campbell

He had been thinking about me. Thinking about us and he knew we could be more, we could have a relationship. I wanted to kick myself for ignoring him for so long. I'd wasted all that time that we could have been together. I set the package on the coffee table. I'd have to look at it later. I needed to get to Campbell even more urgently now.

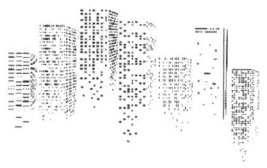

St. Joseph's had to be one of the nicest hospitals in Tampa, but the waiting room still tried to freeze my ass off. The immaculately clean white tile floors and white walls assured me of the sterile environment. The muted flat screen TVs on the walls showed the closed caption running across the bottom, grabbing my attention, though I couldn't bring myself to care about E! News at all.

Our entourage took over one section of blue and gold chairs that were, typically, uncomfortable to wait in. Lorain couldn't sit still and kept getting up and walking around but there was nothing to see, so she'd sit back down. Julien would hold her hand now and then giving comfort only their years of friendship could offer. The smiles between them were slight but knowing. Gavin had slouched down in the chair with his legs sprawled in the isle, his head resting on Tony's shoulder, his eyes closed. Tony's arms crossed over his chest and he'd closed eyes, but he sat up right, tucking his feet under the chair.

Campbell's parents hadn't showed up yet. Lorain had left his mother at her home, where his dad was supposed to pick her up when he'd finished at the police station. We'd been waiting at the hospital for about an hour or two, so I expected they would show up soon.

Campbell had said that his father had not been very nice over the years. I didn't know how much of that I could trust, though, given Campbell's propensity to lie about things. None of the others had given me the impression that Campbell's parents were anything but loving and concerned and they hadn't said anything negative about Campbell. While they didn't embrace me warmly, they didn't exactly give me a cold shoulder or demand that I not be there. I couldn't help wonder if Campbell hadn't made their relationship seem worse than it really was.

I rubbed my temples, staring at the text on the flat screens again. We had a lot to sort out between us, but at the moment, I shoved it all aside. I just needed him to be okay.

Lorain's phone buzzed and she jumped up answering it quickly. "Yes. This is Lorain Montgomery."

Our group all sat up, taking notice and watching her for news.

"Okay...okay...thanks." She hung up and looked at us, smiling brightly. "He's on his way here. They got him. Kristofer Turner has been taken into custody. So Camp will be here in just a few minutes." As if on cue, we heard sirens approaching. I didn't know if that would be him or not, but we all watched the front door as if it were a bell ringing for Pavlov's dogs.

My stomach flipped. Campbell was okay. He may still need medical attention, but he was alive...safe. For the moment, that's all that mattered. I thought that would be enough. Until the paramedics wheeled him in.

As soon as I saw his shock of blond hair, I jumped up and sprinted across the waiting room floor. I couldn't get close to him, but the need had me pushing forward. Someone told me that I'd get my chance to see him and someone else's arms held me back, but I ignored them all. I got a glimpse of Campbell's bruised face: blue, green, and a sickly yellow splotched across his cheek and jaw, visible even under his dark beard that had grown in some. The ugliness of it marred his perfect, delicate features.

Anger bloomed in my chest and I roared, "Campbell!" I needed to touch him, comfort him, and kill the bastard that had hurt him. That destructive impulse drove me and I leapt forward. Campbell's eyes popped open, huge and tawny-brown. He saw me. He smiled, faintly and closed them again.

"Hey, hey!" Gavin clucked in my ear, as he and Tony pulled me back into the waiting room, very much against my will.

"I need to see him."

"Hey, tough guy. He's here. He's fine. Give the docs a minute to check him out. It's going to be fine." Gavin pushed me none too gently into the closest chair.

I buried my face in my hands. I'd really made a fool of myself, but I couldn't help my reaction. Campbell had crawled under my skin. Whether I wanted him there was moot. I needed to make sure he was okay with my own eyes and with my own hands.

The time seemed to really drag on at that point. None of us were allowed to see him and my concern escalated, making my stomach churn.

I texted my boss to let him know the situation. I texted my mom for her support. I stared at the grid of suspended ceiling tiles and fluorescent lighting overhead. All of this in a meager attempt to not think about Campbell and what had happened to him. What that man did to him. I wanted to tear the bastard up like a dog in a fight. It was probably a very good thing that the man had been taken into custody, but it didn't make my instinct to protect Campbell, to avenge him, any less.

At some point, the front doors slid open and Campbell's parents came charging in. They spoke with Lorain briefly and inquired at the desk. After just a moment, they were ushered back behind the wall of honey colored wood. I had no right, but that didn't stop my extreme jealousy all the same. I wanted to be the one holding his hand and comforting him; the one supporting him and giving him whatever he needed.

I groaned and slung my arm over my face. As those feelings and desires rushed over me, I realized that none of his lies mattered. I was a basket case and totally gone for him.

Julien bumped my arm, getting my attention. "Huh?"

He nodded to the doors where Campbell's parents had disappeared. Mitchell Fain stood there, beckoning. For me?

"Go," Julien said, nudging me again.

I stood up, unsure if my legs would really hold me up. "Me?" I asked softly, approaching his dad.

"Yes. He wants to see you. Go on." He walked with me through the room and past a large central desk area where nurses and other personnel, all dressed in colorful scrubs, busied themselves with important medical stuff. Then he directed me farther down the hall before turning and heading back to the waiting room.

I peeked through a curtain partially covering the window of his room and could see two beds, one empty. So I pushed the door open and walked in.

Campbell sat up in the bed, dressed in a hospital gown that made him seem even smaller and more fragile. His mother sat in an armchair that looked a lot like the waiting room chairs, though it might have been more green than blue like the ones there, and held his hand. She had been very quiet and calm through the entire ordeal, even when she'd seemed confused. When she looked up at me, her eyes reflected both sadness and relief at the same time. I could see the features that she'd given her son: high cheekbones and large eyes. Her hair was golden brown, with wisps of gray.

She turned to her son, patted his hand. "I'm going to give you guys a few minutes. Okay? I need something to drink anyway." Her voice was soft and reassuring. She patted my shoulder fondly as she passed me.

"Hi there," Campbell said, his voice hoarse.

"Hi yourself, tiger."

I could see tears welling up in his eyes and his shy face morphed into a painful grimace. "I missed you," he sobbed out.

It took less than two seconds for me to cross the small space and pull him into my arms. "Oh, God! Campbell. I missed you too. I'm so, so sorry."

His arms slowly came around me, as if he was unsure of what he was allowed to do. I pulled back a little and looked at him. "Did they give you something for pain?"

"Yep. Right after they did X-rays. Thought my jaw might be broken, it hurt so fucking much, but nah...just bruised. Thank God."

"My God. What did he do to you? I want to kill him."

Campbell shook his head. "No. It wasn't that bad. I mean,

right, this?" He gestured to his face. "When he first grabbed me I fought him. Once he had me locked down, he was nicer." He shrugged as if that made up for the initial assault.

"I don't care if he's the next Mother Theresa, Campbell. He hurt you."

Campbell rubbed his hands over my arms, soothingly, making me immediately feel guilty.

I stilled his hands. "Hey, I'm supposed to be the one comforting you here."

"God, Stone. You are. Just being here...after everything. When Mom told me how you've been..." Tears rolled down his cheeks.

I couldn't take it. I pulled him close again, a little more careful of his IV this time. "No. Shush. We'll start over Campbell. It's okay. You're okay. We'll work the rest out I promise."

"Why?"

"Fuck! Campbell. You're important to me." I wanted to tell him I loved him, but that L-word scared the crap out of me. After everything he'd just been through, I didn't want to scare him too.

I sat back in the chair, holding his hand. "I want to kiss you, but I'm afraid I'll hurt you."

Campbell smirked. "So, you're taking me back?"

I huffed. "Yes. I am, but you can't lie to me. How do I trust you now? I'm not sure how to work through that yet."

"I only did it so you'd notice me, think I'm something special." His eyes dropped down to his hands. He played with the oxygen monitor they had clamped to his finger and frowned.

"Damn, Campbell, even if you didn't have a job at all and were flat broke and didn't have a rich daddy to rescue you, I'd still think you were something special. You are special. I knew that the first second I laid eyes on you."

Campbell glanced up at me, eyelashes flickering.

"Where are your piercings?" Had that asshole kidnapper taken them?

"I took them out. Before all this." He waved his hand around.

"Why?"

"I'm trying, Stone. No one wants some punk kid with a gauge in his ear and fucked up hair. I have to grow up. It's time." He still didn't look at me directly, and I wanted those brown eyes on me.

"You can't change to please others, Camp."

"What the fuck do you know about it? Seriously, look at you. If I looked like you, I'd have more options. And...I, uh, I think—"

I knew he wasn't mad at me, just feeling sorry for himself, but that shit didn't fly with me. Not anymore. I stood up again. "Campbell, baby. It's okay to change yourself, but do it for you. You can change to please yourself, but don't do it for others. You know? Because you're fine the way you are."

"I guess. But, if I want to get where I want to go, it's going to have to happen."

"Where do you want to go?" I trailed my fingers down his arm, afraid of his answer and maybe that was irrational, but after the last few days, I couldn't imagine living without him in my life.

"I want to be a police officer. The way those guys saved me. Handled the situation. Their confidence. I...I want that."

Even though Campbell's new insight might just be a little bit of hero worship, I wasn't going to dissuade him. "Okay, baby. You can do whatever you want to do. I'm here. Just know that if you're going to be a cop. You really have to tell the truth."

"I get it. And, Stone...I haven't said this yet, but...uh. You know? I'm sorry. Really sorry. I don't want to lose you. Please?"

I held his hand, rubbing my thumb over his. "Of course, tiger. Let's start over. Like I said."

Campbell smiled wide, the happiness reflecting in his eyes and lighting up his face, despite the bruises. He pulled his hand away from me and held it out for a business like handshake.

"Hi, I'm Campbell Fain," he said, as I gave in and shook his hand. "My dad's a hot shot lawyer, but I'm just a hot mess."

23 Campbell

When they finally decided to release me from the hospital I must have looked like a Dali painting with these bruises running down the side of my face in a multi-colored masterpiece. The parts not covered in the unusual pigments stood out paler than I normally appeared, and all of it masked behind dark whiskers because I couldn't bring myself to shave. The contrast had to be vivid.

I wondered why Stone had stuck around. My hair, all tangled and sticking up everywhere, went way beyond bed head. I stunk, needing a shower was an understatement and the first thing I planned to do when I got home. Not to mention the fact that every muscle in my body rioted against me with pain and cramping, as if divorcing my bones.

The detective guy Lorain was goo-goo for confirmed that Kris had indeed hit me with the tire iron, which was why they kept me so long, fearing a concussion. That blow had not been the cause of my jaw pain, though. That was just his fist. *Motherfucker!* The tire iron landed closer to the top of my head; my blond mop probably hid the bruises. I had a nice sized lump there that I hadn't noticed before the medics started checking me out. All that mess packaged in a hospital gown—maybe that's why Stone was still there, checking if my ass was hanging out the back and it was.

When I got the okay, I dressed in clean clothes Julien had brought me: track pants, my favorite old Pokémon tee and a pair of Andrew Christian briefs, because no matter what I look like or wear I have to be fashionable down there! Silly Julien! The minute I got home, the clothes were coming off because that hot shower had my fucking name on it.

Stone followed me out of the ER like a lost puppy. I wasn't sure if he was afraid I'd disappear again or if he wasn't comfortable around my friends and family. He'd unceremoniously spent the last 72 hours practically locked up with them from what they all said, so I hoped the trial by fire would allow him to relax around them. If he was going to be in my life, he'd better get used to them. Julien, Tony, and Gavin were as much a part of my family as my folks. Then there was Lorain. Yes, she was family, but also a more complicated subject. I thought Stone might worry that, since he knew my parents had been playing match maker, but I didn't want anything to do with her girly bits.

My folks met us right outside the ER doors. I eyed my father suspiciously, concerned about what Kris had said. Had he really taken a bribe like that? Was it possible? Since I didn't have the answers, I left it alone. Besides, the possibility of a shower distracted me.

"Camp, sweetie, why don't you come home with us? I'll take care of you," my mom asked before anyone else had a chance to say anything. That kind of stunned me. My mom usually deferred to my dad in most things. Obviously, she sincerely wanted me there, but no way was I going home with her.

"I'm not going to be alone, Ma. I have three roommates and a boyfriend looking out for me." I jerked my thumb to the entourage hanging around.

"But I'm your mother," she protested.

Dad surprisingly chimed in with, "Hun, he's a grown man. Let him alone."

"Thanks, Dad. I think I'm going over to Stone's for a while. We have some, uh, catching up to do. Thanks though, Ma. Everyone." I hugged everyone, ending with Stone and putting my arm around his waist and holding him tight like a life preserver. The exhaustion hit me and I needed out of there and away from everyone, except Stone. "Can we go?" I looked up into Stone's hazel eyes. In the fading sunlight they looked like a soft gray with emerald chips flying around in them, simply mesmerizing.

"Sure. Whatever you need, tiger." With his arm around my shoulders, he gently directed me out to his Honda. I never thought I'd be so happy to see the old thing waiting for me like a friend with its dinged up paneling, but running like a champ under the hood where it counted. Climbing into the passenger seat was like going home.

We didn't really talk much and I fell asleep on the way to Stone's place. I was still groggy as we walked in, but I wanted that shower more than I wanted anything, including sleep or my next meal or air to breathe. "I gotta shower, now. Want to join me?"

"Nah, I'll give you some privacy. Take your time and I'll get some pizza ordered. Can you handle pizza?"

"Pizza sounds so good. You sure you don't want..."

"Oh, I want." He grabbed my hips, his big hands gripping the bones perfectly, as if they'd been made for just that purpose, and yanked me against him. I could feel his dick growing, pressing against my lower abs. "I want more than you could ever know, tiger. I want you. But you're still hurt and this has been a huge ordeal for you. Take a shower. We'll eat. Talk some and then...see how you feel. It's not going to hurt my feelings or break my heart if you just crash. We can get to other things..." He ground his cock against me. "Later. Okay?"

"Yes," I sighed. Even if my feelings wanted to be hurt, seeing how he looked at me, wanting me, but wanting to take care of me more, made them all better. He squashed the self-doubt, leaving me wondrous. I didn't deserve him, but I planned on keeping him and making him happy if I could.

He shoved me toward the bathroom with a kiss on the top of my head and pat on the ass. I didn't protest. I marched into his bathroom and turned the shower on, stripping my clothes off and dumping them on the floor.

By the time I stepped in, the hot water had reached the perfect temperature. Hot succor rushed over me. I used Stone's body wash and shampoo, gently washing my hair twice. I had to get the dust and grime and sweat off of me. Finally, feeling respectable, I got out and wrapped one towel around my waist and the other I threw over my head. I took a moment to use Stone's toothbrush and mouthwash before heading out.

I'd taken a while and Stone had two pizza boxes open on the coffee table when I walked out into the living room. I sat on the edge of the couch and stuffed my face until my jaw ached again and Stone rounded up my pain meds. I swallowed them with a swig of root beer. "They might make me pass out."

"That's okay. I'll put you to bed if you crash on me."

"Thanks."

"You don't have to thank me. I'm so happy you're here. Really, I can't even tell you how much."

I leaned against his side and he wrapped me up in the warmth of his arms. "Stone," I simpered.

"Mm...I've got you," he answered softly, pulling me close.

My hand traveled up along his denim clad thigh. I wanted skin on skin, wanted him. "Please."

Stone's breathing blew heavy and warm down the back of my neck. His hands found my hair, as he pushed me down on the couch. He kissed my temple, very gently, and then my nose. The corners of my lips turned up to a smile at his sweetness, but only for a second, because his lips pressed against them and his tongue slipped inside. I couldn't keep my hips from rolling, grinding against him, searching for friction.

"I've got you," he muttered again, so quietly, I almost didn't hear him.

He cupped the uninjured side of my face and stared into my eyes. In the low lighting they were dark brown with just the few gold flakes catching the light. His dark, silky curls drove me mad and I plunged my hands in them, pulling just a little. I moaned, loving the silky softness. Even the shorter hair above his ears and on the back of his neck danced under my fingertips. "More, Stone."

He kissed me again. Deeply. It meant something, stirring up something inside of me that had never moved before when kissing any other guy. I never wanted to stop kissing him. When he pulled back a little, my eyes darted to his lips and back to his eyes, taking in the sight of him. He skated his index finger across my bottom lip, then gently glided it between my lips and into my mouth. I sucked on it a little, wishing he'd give me more than his finger. He used it to open my mouth so he could get a second finger in there, rubbing them against my tongue. The way he looked at me, commanding my attention, while he fingered my mouth was incredibly erotic.

My hips humped into him, undulating all on their own. The motion flipped an on-switch for Stone. He jumped up, pulling his jersey-style shirt over his head and unbuttoning his jeans, giving me a great view of his bare chest and the bulge not-so-hidden behind denim. His happy trail marched from his belly button down into those open pants, as soft as the hair on his head, and I couldn't help reaching out to touch him, trailing my fingers down the path and into the waist band of his Diesel briefs.

My body lacked in comparison to his. My skin a little too pale and my torso long and skinny, while his golden skin and thick muscled chest left me drooling. I could count the bulging ab muscles, but with his mouth on me, licking at my tiny pink nipples, my brain fuzzed out and I only knew I needed the connection of our bodies touching skin to skin.

Stone's warm hands skimmed down my thighs. "God, I want you."

"I'm here," I responded, breathlessly, as his hands were all over me and finally tugging off the towel around my waist. I lifted my ass to let him pull it away, leaving me lying there naked in front of him. Goose bumps prickled up my arms and legs and pre-cum leaked out of my cock, smearing across my stomach. I didn't have a glorious happy trail for it to get caught in, just a few plain brown hairs that didn't even want to line up right.

Stone pulled his jeans all the way off, dropping them to the floor along with his sexy briefs. I couldn't help notice how manly they were; everything about Stone was manly. If I hadn't met him at a gay club, I never would have thought he batted for my team, but every bit of me was so happy he did. It never hurt to have *out* jocks on the team! He smelled masculine too. Some of that could have been his products that I could smell on myself too, but some of it was just his own natural, earthy scent that I couldn't get enough of.

As I stared at him, waiting for more, his face shifted to something a little less sexy. His brows pressed down, making him appear unhappy or concerned.

"What?"

"Campbell. Listen. I need to know what else you lied about."

I chuckled, nervously. "What?" Why the hell did he bring this shit up now, especially when I thought we'd gotten past it?

"Just...your parents seemed so concerned about you. I can't—I find it hard to believe they have a problem with you being gay. You said you don't get along with them."

"Look. Stone. This peace between my parents and me. At least with my dad. Well, it's probably short lived. I didn't lie about that. The change is new. Very new." I bit my lip unsure of what to tell him, but I'd vowed to be truthful and I'd meant it. I sat up. "I think my dad took a bribe."

Stone plopped down on the couch beside me, but he didn't look at me. "What do you mean?"

"Kris, the guy that did this, kidnapped me? Well, he said his partner died and the hospital was at fault and my dad took a bribe to lose his case."

"Camp. Come on. Your dad is one of the most respected lawyers in town. You don't believe that do you?"

"You don't really know my dad. He's capable of this. Hell, for all I know, his prestige might have been bought and paid for by this kind of corruption all along." I lifted my hand, gesturing to show my sincerity.

"I don't know. That guy was crazy, right?"

"Yes. He was. Total bat shit crazy. He had some kind of break down and I feel bad for him."

"He hurt you," Stone growled.

"Yes, but that doesn't mean... Look—I wouldn't put it past my dad. Any of it. So, don't get used to how cool he's been. I think he threw the case and I think all his nicey-nicey, yeah, that's an act to cover his ass."

"It still doesn't make sense to me. That guy is crazy. He has no grip on reality. I'm not sure you do either."

I ran my fingers through my hair. I should have been more prepared for Stone not to believe me. It did sound odd, but I had to try. "You don't understand, Stone. I'm trying to be real with you. My dad and I not getting along. That's the truth. I never lied about that." I reached out and touched his shoulder. "I, uh, didn't lie about much, Stone. Just my job and school. I wanted to impress you, not become a whole new person."

"But you are, you did. I mean, ugh!" He threw his hands in the air. "Your dad is very well respected. Mr. St. James uses his firm. They were very concerned about you Campbell. When you were missing. They were both devastated. And they never, not once, made me feel like I wasn't welcome there. They understood—"

"Stone." I had to cut him off. "My dad is a first class dick."

Stone stood up. "I don't believe you." He pulled his jeans on and buttoned them up over that gorgeous cock that was no longer hard and ready for me.

"Stone? What the hell?"

"I thought I could do this, but then you say these things about your dad." He grabbed his shirt off the floor. "I don't understand. What I've seen and what I know don't jive with what you're saying. And for you to believe that idiot!"

"Stop. Stop getting dressed. No. I'm telling you the truth. Kris might have—"

"You stop. That man kidnapped you. Beat you. Chained you up. For Christ's sake, Campbell!"

I did not like Stone yelling at me. At all.

I got up and marched back to the bathroom. My own cock had shrunk back up and I didn't know if I could stand to be around him anymore. I couldn't stand to be in his home, smelling him, looking at his things, and looking at him, knowing that's what he thought of me.

I pulled on my briefs and the track pants, but the shirt had gotten wet from being on the floor. I just tossed it over my shoulder, not really giving a damn. It wasn't cold outside. I crammed my feet into my beat up Chucks.

Leaving the bathroom, I headed straight for the front door.

"Wait, Campbell. Where are you going?"

Now he wanted to back pedal? Hell no! I couldn't deal with it. "Home."

"Don't. Let's talk about this."

I wanted to punch him. Punch a wall. Punch myself. "There's nothing left to talk about. You don't trust me. You can't or won't." I shrugged and wrung my shirt in my hands. The floor suddenly had my attention. "I know it's not your fault. I'm mad at myself and that's really the worst fucking thing in the world."

He'd said we could start over, but then he took it back. It crushed me, pulverizing my heart, leaving an aching hole in my chest. When I needed his support the most, he wasn't going to be there for me.

I turned to open the door and heard his soft plea as I walked out. "Don't go."

I didn't know how to gain his trust back. I kept walking, searching for a cab. I'd probably find one once I made it to the heart of Ybor. I could call Julien or one of the other guys, but I didn't even have my cell phone. The cops never gave it back to me and I thought it might be a good idea to get a replacement. I wondered again if I'd find a cab. I wondered if the adrenaline surging through me counteracted the medication I'd taken or if I would end up falling asleep on my feet. I thought about anything and everything I could to distract myself from thinking about Stone and what just happened. I really hated myself and wished Stone would come after me.

He didn't.

24 Stone

I sat on the edge of the couch staring at my front door. *What the hell just happened?* I'd let Campbell walk away from me again. Was this his problem or mine? I chewed at my bottom lip, not knowing what to do and feeling like I'd just been benched during the biggest game of the season.

Dragging my hands through the hair at the top of my head, I got up and searched for my phone. It had fallen on the floor beside the couch. Picking it up, I flipped through my contacts and tapped my mom's entry. I needed someone else's opinion and she had always been my best coach.

"Stone. Why are you calling me? Aren't you with your boyfriend?" She sounded confused.

"No. We just had a fight."

"Already? Maybe this isn't the relationship you think it is."

I sat down with a sigh. "I don't know. He makes me crazy."

"Ah...I see. What did you do?"

I laughed a little, humorlessly. "How do you know *I* did anything?"

"I know you, son." The clattering of dishes came through the phone and I wondered if she were cleaning up from dinner.

"The boys can do that, Mom. I need help here."

"Shh. I'll do what I want."

"Please."

"Fine." I heard more clattering and then it quieted. "What do you need, son?"

"I tried to clear the air between us. Talk to him. You know? About his lies. I needed the truth."

"That was stupid. Didn't you say you were going to let it go?"

"Yes, but—"

"No. Letting it go means letting it go. Not dragging it all back out again. He just went through a traumatic thing, and you're giving him the third degree about stupid shit that doesn't really mean anything. How are you going to have any kind of a relationship like that? He has to be able to trust you enough to tell the truth, Stone. And you need to support him."

"But, he's lying, again."

"About what?"

I sank farther into the cushions of my couch and shifted back and forth between being angry at Campbell and angry at myself. "His father. Why would he do that?"

"What do you mean? What about his father?"

"No, uh, just what he's said about his father and their relationship. I don't know why he thinks his dad is so bad. And he said his father took a bribe, but I don't believe him."

"Are you sure? How do you know?"

She had a point. I didn't really know. I only suspected based on his history and the outlandishness of his story. He knew his father and his capabilities better than me, yet his description seemed incongruent to what I'd witnessed of his father.

"Stone?"

"Yes, Mom. I guess I don't know for sure. Maybe I jumped to conclusions."

"Stupid boy! You need to see him for who he is and stop trying to fit him into your perfect world. Now, fix this."

"Right...I'll figure it out. Thanks, Mom!"

"Love you, Stone."

"You too, Mom. Bye." I hung up quickly, needing to get right to what she'd said—fixing this.

I flipped through my contacts again, this time landing on the number Lorain had given me. She would know more than anyone else.

"Montgomery." Lorain's voice was tight, gruff.

"Lorain. It's Stone."

Her tone softened immediately for me. "Oh, hi. What's going on?"

"I need to ask you some things and I need you to tell me everything. Even if you aren't supposed to."

"Stone...come on," she hissed.

"Seriously. This is about Campbell. Ugh, both of us. As in us, our relationship."

For a minute, I thought she'd hung up on me; the silence rang in my ears. "Lor—"

"Fine." She cut me off firmly. "What do you want to know?"

My heart leapt into my throat, hoping this would get me on the right track, even if it didn't solve everything. "Who is this dude that kidnapped him and what does he have to do with Mitchell Fain?"

I heard a long groan. "You're killing me, Stone."

"It's important or I wouldn't ask. It's—"

"Yes, I get it. It's about Campbell." She huffed a little before going on. "Kristofer Turner was a client of Mitchell Fain."

"And?"

"His partner, Randy Shaffer died in the hospital from some nasty shit that he picked up while he was there, so Mr. Turner hired our firm to look into it and possibly sue the hospital. Mitchell added the doctor and the health organizations that are supposed to keep this shit from happening to the complaint as well."

"Okay. So, he snapped when he lost the case?"

"No, he snapped when he found out about the corruption in one of those organizations and several men on the board stood to lose a lot more than what they could pay Mitchell to throw the case."

"You're fucking kidding me?"

"Damn, Stone. I wish I were. I mean...they didn't think Mr. Turner would be a credible witness because he has a history of mental illness, so they could get away with it, but now that this happened...he may do jail time, but it brought a huge fucking light to this issue. Really, I shouldn't be telling you this."

"I'm not going to say anything. Campbell does need to know, though."

"They're getting ready to make arrests. If it comes out I told you beforehand, I could be disbarred. I can't lose my license, Stone. This is more than likely going to shut our firm down. I'm trying to save jobs here. Including mine! I don't want to be standing on the unemployment line. You get me?"

"Lorain. You mean the world to Campbell. I would never, never do that to you."

"Okay. I trust you, but you have to do something for me."

"What? Anything," I promised, having absolutely no idea what she could possibly want from me.

"Extend that same trust to Camp." How could I refuse that? I'd been the dumbass this time.

"I'm really working on that. I wish you'd talk to him, though. He went through a lot. Talk to him about what happened and about this Turner guy."

"I will. As soon as warrants are issued, I'll call him."

"You're a good friend, Lorain. I was so jealous of you before, but now? I kinda like you."

"Gee thanks. As nice as this chat has been. I have to go."

"Okay, thanks. Bye." I clicked the phone off. Good and bad simultaneously warred within me. Campbell hadn't lied to me, but I didn't believe him. I needed to fix things between us, Mom was right about that. I owed Campbell an apology and I needed to get my head straight around everything. If this relationship could be salvaged, I had to really let the past go, not just say I would, and focus on the present and the future.

I couldn't do anything about it over the next day or two

because I had to work. I'd already taken a few days off when Campbell had been taken and I didn't want to push my luck with my boss. Or maybe I was using that as an excuse, because I didn't know what to say to him.

As the days went by, I didn't call or text Campbell, but he hadn't reached out to me either. My worry about it grew. I was screwing up again and I really need to tell him how sorry I was, but I was afraid that he wouldn't accept that, after all we'd been through.

On Thursday, I got off early and headed to Taco Bus for takeout, then straight over to Campbell's place. Enough was enough, and I was over letting my fear rule me. I knew the longer I waited, the worse it would be, and damn I missed him.

I knocked on the door and Gavin's scruffy mug answered. "He's not here."

Looking around, I only just realized his missing car. "Where'd he go?"

Gavin leaned his hip against the door frame and crossed his arms over his chest. "He took a leave of absence from work and went out to the beach house. Shit's been pretty heavy for him," he accused with his tone, if not the words.

"I know." I held up the Taco Bus bag. "I'm trying here."

Gavin rolled his eyes and took the bag from me. He turned halfway in the door before motioning me to follow with a jerk of his head. He put the food on the counter and ran his fingers through his long, shaggy hair, pushing it out of his face and giving me a better view of his defined features. "Hey." He leaned against the breakfast bar. "You should probably go out there."

I didn't want Gavin's advice on it; I wanted Campbell. I pulled my phone from the pocket of my slacks and speed-dialed him. No answer. "Where's the beach house?"

"Palm Coast." He flipped through his own phone. "Just go. Julien has the address." He tapped his screen and stared at it. "Here." He stretched the phone out to me.

Julien had texted him an address and I immediately entered it into my GPS app on my phone. "Thanks. Enjoy the tacos."

I sat in my car, staring at the address. I couldn't argue with Gavin's logic. I just needed to go out there, but it meant I wouldn't be able to go into work the next day. Or maybe two or three. Maybe, I could take off Friday through to Monday. My mind raced and I couldn't even remember if Mr. St. James had scheduled anything for me over the weekend.

I sucked in a huge breath, fortifying my strength and tapped his contact on my phone.

"Stone. Aren't you done for the day?" he asked instead of saying hello.

"Yes, sir. I need to speak with you, though."

"Okay. Spit it out. What's going on?"

"Uh, I hate to ask, especially on short notice, but I need some time off."

"How long?"

I sucked in another breath. "I don't know, really. It depends on how things go. But this is important, or I wouldn't have asked. I swear."

"It's okay, Stone. Take off whatever you need, but we need a long talk when you get back. We need to discuss your performance and things. So don't plan on taking any time off for some time after that."

"Uh, sure. I mean, I wouldn't take off now. But—"

"I heard you. It's important. I understand. See you in a few days."

"Yes, sir. I'll call you when I get back in town."

"Oh, didn't realize you were going out of town."

I didn't want to tell him any more than I had to and wished I'd kept my mouth shut about being out of town, but maybe that would help me squeeze a few days out of him if I needed it. "Yes, not far, but I have to go. Now."

"Okay. Safe trip." The phone went dead, but it didn't surprise me. St. James had always been very blunt.

I cranked my car up and headed home to pack. My stomach rolled around like a queasy mess. I didn't want to fuck things up at work with St. James. He didn't sound mad really, just concerned, but that was odd in itself. He was normally strict and to the point. If Campbell hadn't meant so much to me, I'd probably have chickened out, but he did mean that much and every fiber of my being needed to get out to the coast and find him.

25 Campbell

Getting my life back together became priority one. I just couldn't slide back in to working the mailroom at Apex after everything that had happened. I needed to be something a little more important than a mail sorter in this world. Not that there was anything wrong with being a mail sorter, but after two years of dealing with other people's mail and a life threatening ordeal, I had to move on.

I kept having nightmares of Kris attacking me, his body heavy on top of mine with a knife to my throat, or a gun to my head. Sometimes he slammed me around. Cement blocks dragged across concrete floors. I woke grasping at my neck, heart pounding like a heavy metal track.

Lorain would tell me to get counseling for it, but I didn't want to talk about what happened. I wanted to move forward. Strangely and against my better judgment, I also wanted to help Kris. Despite his threatening my life, he got a raw deal and my dad helped serve that to him. I blamed my dad more than I blamed Kris.

None of that helped me move forward. None of it helped me with Stone, who I still couldn't stop thinking about. I didn't want him to be the one that got away. I didn't want to think that there could ever be anyone else better for me out there. I needed to show him that I had my shit together, and at the moment, I didn't have anything together. He didn't want this hot mess baking in the Florida sun.

I spent a lot of time walking on the beach and sleeping and reflecting on my world coming undone at the seams. So when a knock sounded on my door, it surprised and irritated me. I knew I wasn't ready to see anybody, especially my fucked up father, and I couldn't think of anyone else that would show up at the beach house. Dad would have used his key, though. The knocking came again.

When I opened the door, my jaw dropped. Stone. He stood there looking sexy with bedroom eyes and a sheepish grin.

"What are you doing here?"

"Julien gave me the address."

I opened the door and let him in, not sure that he'd really answered my question, but I sure as hell wasn't going to turn him away. "Uh, hey. Stone. Uh, I'm kind of fucked up right now."

"You've been drinking?" he asked casually as he followed me into the living room.

"No. That's not what I meant. You want a beer or something?"

"No." He stared at me as if trying to figure me out. Good luck to him. I couldn't figure myself out.

We stood there like that Peeing Guys statue David Cerny did in the Czech Republic, peeing their messages to the world. We were figuratively pissing on each other with our own messages and had been all along. "So?" I asked, needing to get straight to the point before we started the pissing contest up again. "Why are you here?"

He stood there, never looking better in faded jeans and ratty t-shirt. Exhaling loudly, he ran a hand through his messy hair. "Can we sit?"

"Sure." I chose the armchair, still not ready to let my guard down.

Stone sat on the custom made sofa that my mother had ordered from some specialty shop in New York. The rough and sturdy material held up to boys at the shore, but had a light color, making the room feel airy and perfect for a beach house.

Stone looked great there, his fingers fiddling together nervously and looking down at the sun kissed bamboo flooring.

I curled my feet under me and wrapped my hands around my knees to keep from fidgeting. I knew Stone had something to say, or he wouldn't have driven all the way out. Impatience wiggled its way through me and I needed him to get on with it, yet I didn't want to hear it at the same time. I didn't need any more pissing guys in my life. "Listen, Stone. You can stay over. There's a guest room. It's getting late, so..."

"I'm sorry. So, sorry. This..." He gestured between us. "This has all been my fuck up. All of it. My insecurities, my doubts. Not really about you, but about me. And."

"And what?"

"I tend to be unrealistic about things. And I don't know if I can be what you need."

I burst out laughing. His face looked hurt. I didn't want that, but how could this wonderful man ever think he wasn't enough for me? "Stone, my God." I took a breath to calm myself. "Stone, baby. You're more than I could ever want or need. I don't deserve you." I leaned my head back against the chair and closed my eyes. My throat scratched with the remnants of my outburst, but all laughter died away.

Hot lips pushed against my own, fingers moved through the beard on my cheeks, and when I opened my eyes, Stone's perfect face lingered close to mine. I kissed him back, then stopped. We'd had enough of this game. I pushed at his chest and he knelt on the floor in front of me.

"Stone. I have a lot to say to you, but I'm tired. I'm not ready for this."

He nodded, frowning, and rubbing his hot palms on my bare legs. I wanted to spread them and take him in, but I couldn't until we straightened our shit out—because that's how adults behaved and I had to grow the fuck up.

"Let's just sleep on it and talk in the morning? Please."

This time when he nodded, the corners of his mouth lifted into a sweet smile, filled with hope. Yeah, that was there...hope, but I could also see his frustration. "You're such a brat, Campbell. You can't keep running from things."

My mouth dropped open again. Brat? "I'm not fucking running away from anything, Stone. I'm trying to figure this shit out, trying to get my head on straight. I needed time and this is a damn good place to think about it all."

Stone huffed. "Then let's go take a walk. On the beach. We can talk or just walk together and think. Then we can go to bed and talk in the morning."

"You're pushing me."

"Yes, I am. Come on." He stood up and offered me his hand. I took it and let him pull me out of the chair.

"Come on then." I couldn't tell him no. The thought of walking along the beach in the dark, listening to the crash of the waves under the stars with Stone, tempted me past any possible refusals. I slid my feet into my flops and nodded for him to follow me out.

We walked down the boardwalk and stopped beside the water. Stone stopped and pulled off his sneakers and socks and I kicked off my flops so we could walk barefoot through the cool sand. We had the beach to ourselves, no other people around for miles and miles of dark shoreline.

"You stopped shaving." He took my hand and turned me toward him. We couldn't see each other well in the dark, but I could see enough to recognize the longing in his eyes.

"You noticed."

"I like it." He turned and started walking again, our fingers still laced between us. After a few minutes, Stone stopped and tilted his head back. "Fuck! Look at the stars!"

"I know, right. You can see them so much better out here."

I heard his breath suck in when he looked out across the pounding surf, silver beneath the moonlight. "Okay. I am so sorry. This is the perfect place to come and figure shit out. You were right."

"I know." I bumped my shoulder into his and took his hand. We walked along the shore, just out of reach of the water, knowing it would be cool this late at night.

After a few minutes of quietly appreciating the night on the beach, I couldn't take it anymore. "I'm sorry, Stone. If I had never lied to you...Fuck! I don't know. Maybe we'd be in a different place now. I just wanted you to think more of me than I really was and I didn't think it would matter."

"It did matter. From the first second I saw you, I knew you were something more than anyone else in that place. I shouldn't have got my feelings hurt over it, though. And, I told you we'd start over."

"But you didn't. You didn't and you still don't believe me."

"I believe you. I won't doubt you again. But I also won't give any more second chances. If anything else comes up as a lie, we're done. I don't want that. We could have something here, so much more than we've ever had before."

"I think so too. You won't...I won't...I mean, just no more lies. I promise."

"And no more running. I took a few days off but I think my boss is pissed about it. I can't lose my job."

"You shouldn't have." I turned to him, grabbing his shoulders.

"You're more important."

I plopped down, sitting on the ground, not caring about sand in my crack or the icy waves lapping at my toes. No one had ever told me I was more important than a job, a life...anything. I'd never been that important to anyone, not even Julien.

"I have to tell you something," he confessed, settling down beside me.

"What?"

He exhaled loudly. "Not to keep rehashing this, but I do really get why you lied...to start with anyway. I do, because I lied, too."

What? Anger rose, simmering beneath the surface, waiting to explode. How could he have put me through all of that when he'd lied too? "What the hell, Stone?"

"I didn't want to tell you because I've been teased and picked on so much...my whole God damned life. I pretty much put it behind me now, but...uh, if you're going to meet my family, I'd better tell you now."

"Stone?"

"I do have a middle name. I just didn't want you to make fun and I didn't know what you were going to be to me. So, I'm sorry and I get it and I think we both can move on from this, right? Forgive me?"

"What's your middle name?" I actually thought it was kind of funny. I wanted to stay mad, he'd been so hung up on my own little white lies, but it was such a minor thing. "I'm kind of pissed. So...give it up, like now."

Stone groaned and covered his face with his hands. "Rhett," he whispered from between his fingers.

I couldn't help laughing. It might have hurt his feelings but he deserved it. "Stone Rhett Medlock?"

"Yes," he groaned again.

"As in Rhett Butler, Rhett?"

He glared at me and I bumped my shoulder against his.

"This is so funny. I forgive you Rhett, because frankly, I don't give a damn!" I giggled.

Stone huffed, "That's why I didn't tell you." He pulled up his knees, crossing his arms over them and pouted. Actually pouted.

"It's okay," I sighed, once I stopped laughing.

For a few minutes, we just sat together, shoulders and thighs touching, and stared out at the powerful ocean and the endless stars. A bright streak flared and died above us.

"Campbell! Did you see that? What was that?"

"A shooting star."

"Was it? I think that's special."

"I think you're special, too. Please, Stone?" I didn't even know what I asked him for, but he apparently did. He leaned in, cupping my face and probing my beard with his fingertips, and kissed me. This time I wasn't planning on stopping. I let his tongue explore my mouth and wasn't surprised when one of his fingers slid in beside his tongue, making me giggle.

He pulled back and looked at me, then laid back in the sand and rolled me on top of him. I ground my hips into him, looking for some friction and enjoying the way my cock hardened so quickly for him.

Stone's hands explored my back, slipping into the waist band of my board shorts. I leaned back and untied the front, making them looser, but when I went to lie back down on him, he stopped me and yanked my shorts down, exposing my cock. We were going to end up with sand where we didn't want it, but in that moment, I just couldn't be bothered.

"Shuffle back a little, tiger." His big hands guided me as I moved down his thighs, giving him access to unbutton his jean. He shoved them down to the top of his thighs, and I could see he was going commando, because his beautiful cock popped right up for me. I leaned forward, taking it into my mouth and then pulling back off, licking at his head. He groaned a little, tugging at my shoulders. "Come here."

I leaned over him and kissed him, loving his heavy arms around my back, hands grabbing my ass.

"Fuck! Campbell. I want you."

"Yes," I said, sitting up into a crouching position over him. My body still ached from my injuries, making me happy to be on top. "Me too." I lined our cocks up and grabbed them between both hands. Stone held me steady as I stroked our cocks together and rolled my hips a little, fucking against him and my palms. I liked it, but not nearly enough. "Fuck. Let's go back to the house. I need you."

"No. Not yet," he whispered. "Just lick your hands."

I thought he was nuts, but my cock was onboard. I licked both palms, slobbering all over them and went back to jacking us off. There was no stopping at that point. I tightened my fingers and thrust my hips, making my cock drag along his in the tight hold.

Ignoring the sand in his ass and the water lapping at his feet, Stone popped his hips up and down, grunting until his body shook and he came, squirting out over my fingers and cock. That made my grip slippery and the slithery feel set me off, adding my own cum to the mix with my balls pulling up tight and a new shooting star flickering behind my eyelids.

I collapsed against his chest. "Never, never going to forget this night," he gasped.

I agreed with a nod.

"Okay, house now. Let's go get cleaned up."

I had to agree with that too, sand stuck to everything.

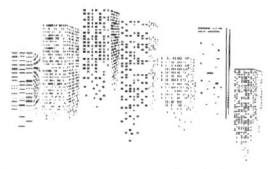

After a quick shower, we crawled into the master bed, naked beneath the sheets. His arms around me made me feel safe. He rubbed my back and wrapped his legs around mine and I cuddled into his chest. It made it easier to open my mouth and say what I needed to say.

"I can't believe we're here. Together. I thought I was going to die in that hangar, Stone."

"I didn't let myself think about that, honestly. I couldn't. I had to focus on them getting you back. I knew you'd be okay."

"I didn't. I don't know how you had that kind of faith, but you weren't there. You didn't see just how crazy he was. I was...terrified. For the first time in my life, I think. Damn! It made things really clear, though. Thinking about my life and what's important. I'm serious about being a cop. It's still law and helping others but it's nothing like what my dad does. I want to make a difference and I want you to be proud of me."

"I'm so proud of you, tiger."

"Huh, I don't know why."

"You made it through that. And instead of falling apart, you're putting yourself back together. Reaching for something more. Something better. Most people? Nah, most people would fall apart, but you didn't."

"I fell apart. You just weren't around to see it."

"So? You picked yourself up."

I sat up and looked into his face, needing to see his reaction. "You're being very supportive for someone that I let down...You know? Not just the lies, but I walked away when I should have stayed to work things out."

"You never let me down, Campbell. Not really. Not in any way that really counted. We both did our share of walking away. So, stop it."

I bit at his lip and he lurched up, taking my mouth and flipping me to my back in one move. "You learn that playing football, big guy?"

Stone's chuckle made my heart pound. "Maybe," he laughed.

"Okay."

He touched my bottom lip with the tip of his finger, then rubbed it over my tongue. "I want you in my life, Campbell Fain. Every way I can have you. Don't think I'll ever get tired of exploring you." I noticed his hips grinding into me as he spoke, and his cock was already hard again, poking into my upper thigh.

"I'm here. I'm yours."

"Can I make love to you, Campbell? Are you ready for that?"

I nodded briskly. "Please," I breathed out, proving my words with my own cock, grinding into his stomach.

"You have, you know, stuff?"

I bit my lip. I hadn't brought anything with me. I didn't think Stone would track me down. "No."

"Well, I do." He wiggled his eyebrows. "I had a good feeling about this." He jumped up and grabbed his jeans, pulling them on. "It's out in my car. Can I bring in my bag?"

"Uh, yes. You're staying with me, right?"

Stone smiled and dashed out the door, leaving me in that big bed with a raging hard on and a fiercely pounding heart.

26 Stone

I hadn't run that fast since playing high school football, but I couldn't possibly get my shit out of the car and back in the house fast enough. My cock strained against the zipper of my jeans, begging to be set free, begging to find Campbell's hole. I needed to connect with him, to be inside him. I imagined I could hear my cock yelling, "Now-now-now!"

The door slammed behind me, and I rushed to the . Campbell was sprawled out over the bed, his eyes closed and hands behind his head, elbows poking out. His creamy skin against the peach colored sheets made me drool a little. His cock stood at attention, lurching away from his body, as if trying to get to me.

I dropped my bag and pounced on him, totally losing control. His cock rubbed against my tongue, filling my mouth as I enveloped him, pulling up and down, up and down. I flicked my tongue across his head, down the length of his cock, and all around his balls. I sucked one gently into my mouth while I tongued it, making Campbell squirm and dig his fingers into my scalp.

"Stone, please," he moaned.

I stood up and shucked my jeans to the floor. I took a minute to find the supplies I'd tucked into my bag—just in case—and tossed them on the bed, before climbing up Campbell's naked body. I reveled in the skin to skin contact with him, loved how he squirmed underneath me, loved the slide of his body against mine, and the friction of the hair on our legs rubbing together. "Campbell..." I wanted all of it, all of him. I kissed his rose tattoo with open mouth and tongue.

"Get me ready. I can't wait much longer. Need. Need you."

It only took a moment for his legs to spread and bend at the knees, feet flat on the mattress beside his butt. I flicked open the cap on the Astroglide tube and squirted it over my fingers and dripped it down his balls and ass, just to see him squirm again.

"Stop," he called out, making me laugh. "God, just do it, Stone."

He was my ideal of sexy, with thin, firm thighs, long and sleek abdomen, and his exposed hole, vulnerable just for me. My fingers slid inside him and he lifted his ass to take more. I jacked his cock a bit as I played with his ass, watching my fingers work in and out, prying him open.

"Stone," he growled out, bucking against my hand.

"I know, tiger." I kissed his knee and he shivered for me.

We still hadn't defined this thing between us, but I knew that we had something more, different than ever before. When he looked up at me and licked at his dry lips, my heart fluttered and my chest rumbled and ached like that old Dr. Seuss story about the Grinch whose heart grew three sizes too big when he realized Christmas wasn't about material things. For sure, this thing between us was about something intangible and existed even without the sex, but that made it even better. I loved him for the looks he kept giving me, for the laughter on his lips, for the way my insides melted when he touched me, and for the way he just kept trying, no matter what. Campbell never gave up, not really, even when he thought he had every reason to let go. I had to give him that same thing back.

When I finally leaned back to roll the condom down my cock, I was more than ready to show him what I had, but before I could line my head up to his hole, he sat up. "Stone?" He gave me a questioning look.

"Huh?"

"I don't want to keep going back and forth over this. I want you, but sex isn't going to help us figure it out."

"You're stopping now?" His cock poked up, just as hard and heavy as mine, and I was relieved when he laughed and tackled me, throwing himself in my arms.

"No. Not stopping. Just checking in."

I wrapped my arms around him and shifted us around, so he straddled me, and I sat on the edge of the bed. "Lift up," I whispered my command, but he listened, understanding where I directed him. As he slowly sank down on my aching dick, I spoke against the sweaty skin of his neck. "Campbell. I love you."

Campbell made low noises in his throat, a cross between a moan and a whimper, as he completely seated himself on my cock. "God, Stone, love you, God," he muttered as he slowly moved up and down, fucking himself on my cock. He grunted another, "Stone."

His tight heat overwhelmed me. I met his thrusts, held him and helped him move with one hand on his ass and my other arm around his waist. Our motions were leisurely, grinding against each other at a forced pace that spoke of wanting the moment to last and of making love. Sweat dripped down his back and he shivered. His lean thighs worked as he pushed up and down.

"Oh, God. Feels so good, Stone," he panted and tossed his head back with another throaty groan. I couldn't take it anymore.

I needed to fuck him fast and hard. I flipped us over and pushed his legs up and out, hands on the back of his thighs. I leaned down to kiss him, quickly exchanging tongues.

His big eyes stared up at me, needy and passionate. "Now, yes...do it...fuck!"

I pushed hard and fast, knowing I wouldn't last. I didn't think Campbell would either. Our skin slapping together rang out in the otherwise quiet room, followed by our grunting, panting, and moaning.

Campbell's moans were peppered with curses coming from his sinful mouth. I had to taste him. My mouth came down on his throat and I sucked up a mark before licking down his collarbone. It made him hiss and sigh. Salty sweat tingled on my tongue and his noises reverberated on my lips.

"Fuck me! So good, Stone. Fuck. God!"

"Mmm...so close."

Campbell trembled and cried out as he came, tightening his ass around my cock as he shot out between us. "Stone," he groaned and his big puppy eyes closed tight. His noises and expressions and clinging ass threw me into my own orgasm. As my balls pulled up tight, that tingling danced through my body and tiny white fireworks sparked in the upper corner of my eye as I shook out the last of my cum.

I leaned to the side and collapsed on the bed beside him. His fingers dragged lazy trails through the cum on his stomach. I couldn't move if I wanted to.

"Campbell, tiger," I huffed, still out of breath, but needing to get the words out, almost as much as I needed his mouth again. "I meant what I said. I love you. Everything else...well, it'll work out." I stretched over him, and took his mouth, shoving my tongue inside, not wanting to wait for any other response from him.

27 Campbell

My toes dug into the cool sand and the ocean water splashed over my legs. Spending time with Stone at the beach was probably one of the happiest times in my life and I wanted those two days to last forever.

Stone lingered up at the house, packing the cars. He had to go back to work and I still had a lot of things to sort through. I knew we couldn't hide forever, but a few more minutes with my face in the sun, smelling the salty air as it breezed over my shoulders couldn't hurt.

I heard Stone holler, "Hey!" right before he grabbed me around the waist and lifted me off of my feet, spinning me around and dragging me out into the water. He threatened to dunk me in and I tried to climb over him to get away, but he wrestled me down. The water splashed up around us and in minutes we were laughing too hard to fight any more.

There were other people on the beach, but no one paid any attention to us. Stone pulled me closer, nuzzling under my ear. "Mmm...cars are packed. Let's shower and nap and maybe shower again before we go." He teased me with kisses along my neck.

I shivered with goose bumps, as he kissed me and I agreed to his plan, but as soon as he stepped away from me, I splashed him, kicking up water, and then I ran the other way knowing he'd chase after me and he didn't disappoint. He caught up quickly and lifted me off my feet. I kicked at the air, but I wasn't getting away this time.

"Stop it, you," he growled in my ear, which made my cock hard.

"Okay, okay. I give up!"

Stone sat my feet back down on the sand. His hands slid from my waist, up my stomach and over my chest. I turned around and jumped in his arms again, wrapping my legs around his waist. He kissed my forehead and my cheeks and my eyes, making me giggle. My heart soared, light as air and for the first time, I didn't doubt him or myself.

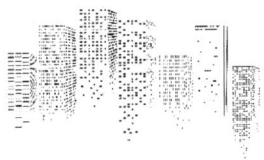

We drove to Stone's house with his promise that I could do some laundry before going home the next day since I was about out of clean clothes. We ordered pizza and played Xbox, just chilling out, until Stone paused the game. I turned to look at him and his eyebrows were pinched down in a scowl.

"What? Oh, God...what'd I do?"

"Nothing. I just don't want you to leave tomorrow."

I shrugged. "I don't have to." I probably would have given in to whatever he asked at that point, but I really didn't want to leave either. Spending another day with him sounded just fine to me.

Admitting that didn't stop Stone's scowling. "So don't. Ever. Stay with me. Live with me."

"What are you saying?"

"I'm saying I want you to move in here. Live with me. Can't that be a part of your new plan?" His serious face slid into a softer expression.

I laughed softly. "Are you pouting?"

"Maybe."

I leaned over and hugged him, my arms around his shoulders. "Okay." I didn't want to leave either. We still needed to talk about logistics and the police academy and how our lives were going to change and merge, but in that moment, that simple agreement was all both of us needed.

He pulled me in closer and kissed me hard. I kissed back, loving our tongues winding together just like we were about to do with the rest of our lives.

"Thank you," he said softly, pushing my hair out of my face.

"I'm cutting that tomorrow. Still want me to live with you?"

"Yes." Another kiss to the forehead.

"I'm not putting my piercings back in. Still want me to live with you?"

His tongue tickled along the ridge of my ear. "Yes. I don't care."

"I'm still going to be a cop. Still—"

"Yes. Yes. I don't care what else you do. Just live here and love me."

"I do love you, baby."

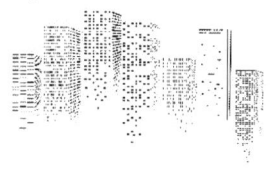

The next day Stone went to work and I did laundry. Blah! Then I called Lorain. I really needed information. She screeched when she answered the phone. "Campbell!! How are you, baby boy?"

"Uh, fine. Calm down, Lulu."

"Mm...don't call me that. Hey? Where are you? Still hiding at the beach?"

"No. I'm at Stone's—well, our place. I'm moving in with him."

"*OhmyGod*! That's fabulous. Have you told anyone else that?" She was overly excited about it and squealing so loud I had to pull the phone away from my head.

"No. I haven't spoken to anyone about anything. I kind of needed to talk to you first, bug."

"Okay. Spit it out. What do you want to know?"

"You know me too well." I bit at an aggravating cuticle.

"Yeah, I do. So?"

"I want to know about my dad and Kris Turner and what's going to happen."

"Are you sitting down?" she asked with a huff.

"Uh, yes. Please, Lorain. I need—"

She interrupted me. "I know. I know. This is just hard. Dad and I have been working to close the practice and transfer clients to a new entity, but we've had to be quiet about it. And, we're trying to do it so we can keep most of the employees, too. Ugh. You've know idea. Anyway, they've issued a warrant for your dad's arrest and they'll probably pick him up this evening. He knows. He's not fighting it."

"He's guilty then?" I knew the answer already. I had known that answer when Kris still had me chained to a brick. I didn't want to believe it of my dad. He was a dick, yeah, but a criminal?

"Looks that way."

"This is going to sound stupid or sick or something, but I'm really feeling for Kris. He didn't deserve this. You know it pushed him over the edge. Losing his partner and then this shit with my dad. The guy's nuts, but like, it's my dad's fault. At least some of it."

"Camp. It's not your fault."

She might have been getting aggravated with me, but I had to stand my ground on this one. "I know that, but I have to do something anyway. What can I do to help him?"

I could hear papers shuffling around in the background. "Don't know, but I guess I should have expected this from you though."

"Whatever." I wondered if she could actually hear my eyes rolling.

"Well, I'll get back to you on that one. I think he'll get hospitalized instead of jail time in light of everything."

"Okay. Good."

"Let's keep in touch baby boy!"

"Of course, bug. By the way, what's the name of the new firm going to be?"

"Montgomery, Montgomery and Forsyth. Lawyers aren't creative much."

"That means they're making you a partner though." I was happy for her. "Congrats! Way to go Lulu!"

"Don't call me that, but really, thanks and back at you. Hang on to that big guy. I like him."

"Me too."

We hung up quickly after that. I spent the rest of the day finishing laundry and getting my ducks in a row so I could apply to the police academy. Life was going to change quickly and I needed to prepare to hang on with both hands.

28 Stone

One year later...

"They're going to be here any minute. Is everything ready?" Campbell asked for the millionth time. His excitement floated around him like living electricity as he bounced up and down on his toes. I just shook my head. I was so proud of him. I would endure any torture for him, even this huge graduation party for him and his fellow police academy graduates that had been a pain in my ass to organize.

It hadn't been an easy time for him, but Campbell never gave up. That was my man...looking at me with puppy dog eyes one minute and sinking his teeth in the next. "Calm down baby. Everything is under control."

His mother and Julien helped me pull the party off. I got the warehouse space from Mr. St. James and I even expected him to show up. He'd given me a fabulous promotion after Campbell and I worked everything out. He'd thought I was leaving him, bored and moving on. Once I reassured him that wasn't the case, work improved. He included me in a lot more of his business dealings and now he was talking about giving me another raise because I'd really worked hard over the past year. I couldn't sit back and coast when I saw how hard Campbell worked for what he wanted. His success had me enrolling in school for business with the support and approval of Mr. St. James as well. He figured that I'm a good investment. I just wanted to make Campbell proud.

People arrived and mingled in the open space. There were tables spread out and covered with gauzy table cloths and fat pillar candles set in trays filled with nuts and bolts, so it would look manlier. Overhead, a hundred single bulbs hung from the ceiling at different levels, giving off a soft white glow, yet still looked industrial. I didn't know how Julien made that happen, but it looked absolutely magical. The overall setting came off as rugged and masculine, but with a low key feel to it and soft touches that took the edge off.

One of those touches had Gavin and Tony acting as bartenders. They both wore cargo shorts that hugged their asses with work boots and socks and tight tank tops, topped with bandanas around their necks. They looked like sexy construction workers. Gavin came off as the bad boy with his longer, sandy colored hair and Tony looked like the boy next door with his short cropped hair and sweet smile. I figured they'd make good tips. Hopefully, Tony wouldn't be gabbing about useless statistics or analyze every drink as he poured.

I sat back and watched Campbell mingle. I loved watching him flitting around talking to everyone. He had changed a lot since we'd first met. He had replaced that sexy swagger and bad boy front with a mature, confident young man, who was sexier than ever. He stopped dying his hair, leaving it a natural honey-brown and cut it military style, and I loved to run my hands across his head, that softness tickling my palms and fingers. True to his word, he never put his piercings back in, but he was still my bad boy when he took his clothes off and I got to lick and touch that tattooed skin.

"Stone!" Lorain yelled across the room and held up drinks in both hands. I smiled and joined her at a table near the front of the room.

"Hey, girl. It's been too long," I said, relieving her of one of the drinks. I took a long swallow and sat next to her, enjoying the soft tingly burn of the alcohol running through me. "What's new?"

Lorain snorted. "Not much. Same shit. Different day."

I lifted my eyebrows. I'd gotten to know her a little and suspected she was keeping something from me. "Lorain?"

"Yeah. I just found out that Camp has been visiting Kristofer Turner...a lot. He's been going there with Gavin."

"Should we be concerned about this?"

Lorain shrugged and sipped at her drink. I waited for her to give me more information. "He has a hearing coming up. It may be about that. But..."

"What?" I leaned in, as if waiting on the latest gossip, but this wasn't just gossip. Something was going on and Campbell hadn't told me about it.

"I don't mean to start shit. I'm just worried that Campbell still has healing to do from what that man did to him...emotionally. You know? He doesn't always show that on the outside."

That I knew was a fact. "Yes, but what? It doesn't seem to be hurting him. Look at him."

"I don't know. Maybe it's helping him. Maybe if Kris gets out...I don't know. It'll be alright, right?"

I stood up. "I need another drink."

Lorain grabbed my arm, stopping me. "Just talk to him, okay?"

"You got it." I grabbed her hand, removing it from me, but kissed her knuckles before letting it go and heading to the bar. The one Gavin tended.

"Hey dude!" Gavin greeted me, but then he saw my frown and his smile dropped. He looked down at his hands and fucked around with the glasses in front of him, as if he were feeling guilty. "What can I get you?"

"You can tell me what you and Campbell have been doing visiting Kristofer Turner?"

"Look, Stone. This isn't the time. You should talk to Camp, anyway."

"I intend to, but thought you could help, since this is a kind of big night for him."

Gavin tossed his head to get the long bangs out of his eyes. "I can get you a drink."

"Fine," I scoffed. "Rum and Coke."

I leaned on the bar while Gavin mixed the drink—it looked like a double. "It's personal," he said, pouring a little Coke on top of the alcohol.

"What is?"

"This thing with Kris. It's personal."

"Personal how?" Irritated with the whole Kris Turner issue that I'd thought we had behind us, my patience waned. I wanted answers.

Campbell's dad did thirty days and had a huge fine and some restitutions to Kris along with his probation that was almost over. The health organizations involved also had fines and restitutions and a few of the board members did jail time and are no longer on the board—early retirement. Right. So, why was it all bubbling back up now?

"I mean, personal for me." Gavin slid the drink across the bar and moved to help the next person.

Campbell popped up next to me. "It's nothing. We'll talk about it later. Okay?" His big brown eyes peered up at me and he lifted that one eyebrow in that way he had.

I couldn't help but smile, as I leaned over and kissed his forehead. "Okay, tiger. I'm just worried about you."

He smiled brightly. "I know, but this time it isn't about me." He glanced at Gavin with a sly smile, and pulled me away from the bar. "Kris has come a long way. He's on meds. He's doing his time and Gavin kind of made friends with him. For me, it's just seeing that he's going to be okay when he gets released in a few weeks."

"If, Campbell. If, he gets released."

"I'm sure he'll be released. With continued care that my dad and his cronies are paying for."

I sucked down my drink and deposited the empty glass on a table while following Campbell to the dance floor. I'd let the situation go for now. It seemed like Campbell was handling it in an appropriate way. Except for the not telling me about it part. We'd deal with that later, though.

A bunch of the people from his class chanted, "Camp,

Camp, Camp!" when we walked out. He high-fived a bunch of them. Then with the music blaring, he focused on me. Exactly where I needed him to be.

We were going to be just fine.

The End

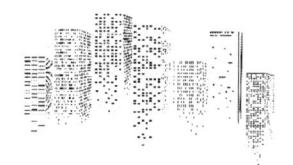

Bonus Scene...

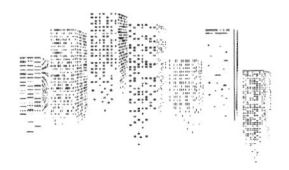

I sat on the edge of the bed fumbling around with the metal hand cuffs. I slapped them against my ankle, letting it cinch tight then using the key to release them, practicing. Again.

I'd be hitting the streets the following week and really needed to be confident I could use them on someone properly. I repeated my assault on my ankle, happy they worked on my thin ankle, but I really needed another person.

"Campbell." Stone.

My heart still leapt into my chest when he came home. "In here." I got up and stood near the door. Waiting.

He pushed it open and stepped through. I grabbed his arm, slapping the cuff on his wrist and wrangled it behind his back.

"What the—?"

"Ah-ha. Gotcha." I grabbed his other arm before he could figure it out and slapped that wrist into the other side of the handcuffs. "On your knees, perp!"

"Perp? What the hell, Campbell?"

I leaned in and nudged my nose under his ear and whispered, "I need practice."

"The fuck you do." He pulled, as if to get away, but I held

his shoulder and shoved him to his knees. "This is crazy. Let me go, Campbell."

"That's Officer Fain to you." I circled round him and leaned in to kiss his forehead. "I'm taking advantage of this...so...be a nice boy and I might let you go, but if you're bad..." I wiggled my finger in front of his face. "I'll have to bring you in."

"I don't think this is how it's done, Campbell." A little smirk burst out of his dark scowling frown. I knew I had him about where I wanted him.

"It is with you." I unbuttoned my cargo shorts, letting them fall from my slim hips. That's when Stone laughed. I stood in front of him wearing a sexy pair of tight, barely covering the cock, briefs—in neon pink.

I tugged my t-shirt over my head and tossed it at him. "What?"

"No matter what you're doing." Stone shook his head. "You have to be wearing the absolute most outrageous—"

"Sexy."

"Underwear."

"You love them." I slid them down my thighs and his eyes followed. Seeing how much he still wanted me gave me a thrill like nothing else. Even shooting bullseyes on the target range.

"I do. I love you. Everything about you."

"Good. Now suck my cock like a good perp, or I'll have to drag you down to the station and book you."

"Yes, sir, Officer Fain, sir."

I moved closer and slid my cock between his gorgeous, made just for me, lips. "Mm...you're so good at this."

Stone moaned something around my cock, but I had no idea what he tried to say. I didn't care either—just that it felt so good vibrating along my shaft. "Gah! Stone. Stop." I had to pull out to keep from coming. I wanted to play around a lot more than that. "Get up," I growled at him, using my most authoritative voice, something else I had to practice.

I helped him to his feet and shoved him around the room,

maneuvering him just the way I wanted him. I unfastened his belt and slacks and tugged them off. He stepped out of them and I tossed them over the chair with all the rest of the clothes we intended to hang back up but never got around to. Then I pushed his bare ass down on the bed and dropped to my knees in front of him.

"My-my, this is a pretty impressive weapon you have, perp."

Stone grunted as I flicked my tongue over his crown. I loved the salty taste of his pre-come. I flattened my tongue and dragged it up the length of him, making him moan.

"Very interesting interrogation technique you have there, Officer Fain."

"Yes! You will talk...and moan...and scream my name."

Stone chuckled for a second, but the sound turned into a moan as I slid my mouth over his cock, sucking and tonguing him, just how I knew he liked it best.

His body shifted around as I worked him over, but with his arms still cuffed and me leaning over him, pushing on his thighs, he couldn't really move his hips like he wanted to. He growled out in frustration.

"Well, now, Mr. Medlock, I think we need to do a cavity search and see what else your hiding."

Stone merely grunted, as I flipped him over onto his stomach. I shoved his legs farther apart and grabbed the lube off the table. He gasped when I squirted it directly onto the sensitive skin behind his balls, letting it drip over them and his crack. I stopped and pulled his ass cheeks apart, rubbing lube between them and down to his hole.

"You're making a mess, Campbell."

I smacked his ass. "Anything can and will be used against you." I slid my finger inside his hole.

"Fuck! You're in a feisty mood...uh, sir, uh, Officer Fain."

I bit his ass cheek where I'd just smacked it, then licked over the red mark I'd left. "I want you, so fucking bad."

Stone pushed his ass up higher like a silent offering. One I would enjoy taking. I rubbed slick fingers over his balls and his cock and up to his ass then quickly worked him over, loosening him up, before grabbing my cock, making sure it had enough lube on it. "I'm so hard for you, Stone. Gah! You ready?"

"Fuck, yes. Do it."

I smacked his ass again, this time on the other cheek. "Mouthy, boy. You'll end up in the slammer for sure."

"I'll end up being slammed by you for sure. Just do it. Officer Fain."

I couldn't stop myself from laughing at his fake insolence, or pushing the head of my cock into his asshole. It breached the muscle with groans from both of us. I slid in slowly and stopped once my hips pushed up against his ass. Stone's forehead rubbed against the sheet and if his hands had been free, they'd have been clawing at them, but they weren't. They were deliciously cuffed behind his back.

My cock twitched, involuntarily. Stone moaned again, so I slowly withdrew, canted my hips to a better angle, and slid back in.

"Oh, Fuck, Campbell!"

"Yep. That's what it's called baby."

"Gah! Fuck me now, baby."

I didn't wait any longer. I thrust forward, grabbing Stone's hips, pulling him toward me as I plunged inside him.

"Harder, Campbell, faster." Stone's words panted out, muffled by the mattress.

I gave him what he asked for. My grip tightening, my hips pumping, my thighs working, my dick tingling. Stone's hole clinched, tightening, his heat on my flesh, scorching. Sweat dripped down his back, some from him and some from me, mingling, just as we were—connected and together. Everything just right.

"Ah!" My whole body tensed up, paralyzing, as I came.

Stone's ass gripped me tighter, knowing I was coming and milking every bit of it from me, until I fell over him.

"Ow! Campbell, please."

I crawled off him, reluctantly. I didn't want to separate.

That moment when my dick slides out, free again in the world, would always be a little heartbreaking. My dick wanted to be safe inside Stone's ass, always, no matter how impractical. I didn't want Stone to suffer though, so I got up. "Shit! Where'd I put the keys?"

"Oh, fuck no! Get these off of me now, Campbell. Damn you." His tough words gasped out between bouts of laughter.

"Calm down, big guy. I've got them." I rummaged around the floor, finding my shorts and the key tucked in the pocket. I unlocked the cuffs and rubbed Stone's arms and shoulders. "You okay?"

"No," he groaned and turned over, sitting up on the bed. I could instantly see the problem. His cock stretched up, hard with a gentle inward curve, almost reaching his belly button.

"Damn, I'm a selfish lover."

"No, you're not. Now finish me."

I could tell Stone had had enough of our game, although it had obviously turned him on as much as it did me. I'd have to put him out of his misery, though. Not that I wouldn't enjoy it.

His cock was shiny and slick from the extra lube I'd used, so I pushed his shoulders back on the bed and cuddled up next to him. Taking his cock in hand, I stroked him long and slow.

"Stop that, Campbell."

"You know if feels good."

"Too good, and I'm past getting wound up. Make me come."

I huffed at him and sat up. He wanted immediate release, so I gripped him hard with one hand, stroking fast, while I massaged his balls with my other hand, rolling them around. He moaned, appreciatively, so I knew I hit the mark. In seconds, he blew his load, making me jump in surprise at how quick he shot off.

He sighed and covered my hand with his, stopping my motions. "That was good. Thank you, Officer Fain."

"Any time, baby."

"Yeah? I kind of like this game, tiger. Maybe next time I

can be the cop?"

"In your dreams! I'm the cop!"

We giggled together, Stone pulling me close to his chest. "You can be whatever you want, tiger. I'll always be right there with you."

I stretched my head up and kissed him and he rubbed his hands through my short cropped hair. "I love you Officer Fain."

"Aww...I love you too, perp."

Evasive Maneuvers Playlist

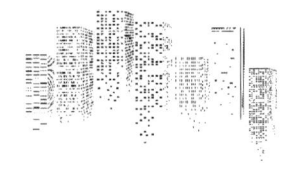

Dedicated to my readers – thanks for contributing!

Quarterback, Kopecky
Things Happen, Dawes
Breaking Up My Bones, Vinyl Theatre
The Writing's on the Wall, OK Go
Hollow Moon (Bad Wolf), AWOLNATION
Lydia, Highly Suspect
Tear in My Heart, Twenty One Pilots
Get Over It, OK Go
My Body, Young The Giant
Out of the Black, Royal Blood
Young and Unafraid, The Moth and the Flame
Mercy, Muse
Lie Love Live Love, AWOLNATION
Sic Transit Gloria...Glory Fades, Brand New
Underdog, You Me At Six
More Than Gravity, Colin & Caroline
Iris, The Goo Goo Dolls
eez-eh, Kasabian
Need You Tonight, INXS
The Hollows, Why?
Black Velvet, Alannah Myles
Tear You Apart, She Wants Revenge
Rocky Mountain Way (cover), Godsmack
A Little Bit More, Dr. Hook
Ghost Town, Adam Lambert
Temple, Kings of Leon
Baby Don't You Lie to Me, The Fratellis
Extraordinary, Prince Royce

Evasive Maneuvers Playlist Continued...

Sparks, Hilary Duff
Ho Hey, The Lumineers
Moonlight, Hanni El Khatib
Emotional Rescue, The Rolling Stones
Beast of Burden, The Rolling Stones
Sex and Candy, Marcy Playground
R U Mine?, Arctic Monkeys
Circus, Brittany Spears
Bad Dream, The Mowgil's
Iron Moon, Chelsea Wolfe
Get It, Matt and Kim
Love You Madly, Cake
Inside Out, Eve 6
Hard to Say I'm Sorry/Get Away, Chicago
2 Heads, Coleman Hell
Lover, Please Stay – Live, Nothing But Thieves
Rebellion (Lies), Arcade Fire
Figure It Out, Royal Blood

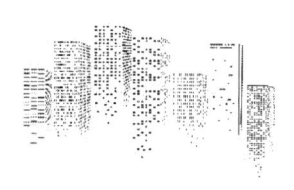

ABOUT THE AUTHOR

Lynn Michaels lives and writes in Tampa, Florida. When she's not writing, she enjoys kayaking, drinking sangria and enjoying the sunshine. Looking at things from a different point of view and bringing a twisted outlook to her writing keeps things interesting and new.

Lynn can be found hanging out on Facebook and other social media spots...

https://www.facebook.com/Lynn-Michaels-1450504665203028/

https://rubiconwriting.com/lynn-michaels/

Lynn also supports LGBT charities and support groups

Cyndi Lauper's fund to fight LGBT youth homelessness

https://truecolorsfund.org/

Trevor project info:

http://www.thetrevorproject.org/

Special Thanks and Disclaimer:

This is a work of fiction. Any similarities to the real world are imagined. All brand names are used with the utmost respect and are either creations of the author's imagination or used fictitiously. This is not an actual representation of Tampa, or any company or organization that may or may not be located there. Facts and details may have been changed or modified for use in this particular plot for the purposes of creating interesting fiction. This is an erotic mm romance with 18 and older type scenes.

Brand Recognition:

Old Navy, Chubbies, Chucks – Converse All Stars, American Eagle, 2Xist, Xbox – Call of Duty, Nike, Cheetos, BMW – 320i, Honda, Diesel – Umbr-Andre, Armani, Seven Jeans, Taco Bus, Tampa Lightning, Corona, Malio's, Nintendo, McDonalds, Tylenol, Tramadol, Psycho – Norman Bates, E! News, St. Joseph's Hospital, Dahli, Andrew Christian, David Cerny, Astroglide, Dr. Seuss – The Grinch that Stole Christmas, The Rock – Dwayne Johnson,

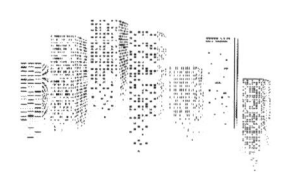

Other Work by Lynn Michaels:

Novellas

The Universe series:
#1 – Elementals
#2 – Disguises

Shot The Plot

Novels:

The Holeshot
Lines on The Mirror
Wanton

Coming Soon:

Cupid's Christmas Arrow (A Christmas Novella)
Holeshot 2

Made in the USA
Charleston, SC
15 July 2016